Deputy of
VIOLENCE

G·K
Hall
&Cº

Also by Ray Hogan
in Large Print:

The Copper-Dun Stud
Day of Reckoning
The Doomsday Marshal
   and the Mountain Man
The Hell Road
Killer on the Warbucket
Legend of a Badman
A Marshal for Lawless
The Outlawed
The Peace Keeper
Soldier in Buckskin
Texas Guns
The Whipsaw Trail

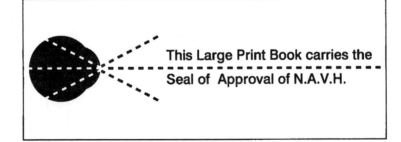

This Large Print Book carries the
Seal of Approval of N.A.V.H.

Deputy of
VIOLENCE

A Shawn Starbuck Western

Ray Hogan

G.K. Hall & Co. • **Thorndike, Maine**

Copyright © 1971 by Ray Hogan

Published in 1999 by arrangement with Golden West Literary Agency.

G.K. Hall Large Print Western Series.

The text of this Large Print edition is unabridged.
Other aspects of the book may vary from the original edition.

Set in 16 pt. Plantin by Minnie B. Raven.

Printed in the United States on permanent paper.

Library of Congress Cataloging in Publication Data

Hogan, Ray, 1908–
    Deputy of violence : a Shawn Starbuck western / by Ray Hogan.
      p. cm.
    ISBN 0-7838-0438-5 (lg. print : hc : alk. paper)
    1. Large type books. I. Title.
  [PS3558.O3473D397   1999]
  813'.54—dc21   98-31641

Deputy of

VIOLENCE

☆ 1 ☆

Shawn Starbuck swung his horse down into the brush-filled cup behind a shoulder of rock and dropped silently from the saddle. He didn't know if the oncoming copper warriors were Comanche or Kiowa. He'd been warned he'd likely encounter both in that blistered, hellish wasteland of west Texas, and that he'd best keep a sharp eye out if he hoped to stay alive.

Crouched, feeling the fiery lash of the sun on his back and neck, praying the sorrel would make no sound, he watched the painted riders wind slowly up the hill. Fourteen in all. . . . About half carried rifles — mostly single-shot, Army Springfield carbines. Evidently they were returning from a raid. Several exhibited wounds, all appeared dog-tired, were slumped heads low, legs dangling loosely, as they sat their lean ponies.

Halfway up the grade one of the braves buckled, fell to the scorched sand. The column came to a halt. The Indian behind the fallen brave rode in closer, stared at his comrade. After a time he dismounted, and saying something in quick Spanish, nudged the man with his toe. There was no response. Others then

7

moved in, and for a time all carried on a conversation in the seemingly angry but normal manner of their kind.

A decision was reached. The brave *was* dead, and the question, obviously, had been whether to leave him for nature to dispose of or take him on to the village. The latter proved to be the choice. They draped the limp shape over a horse, tied feet to hands under the animal's belly, and moved on.

Slowly, painfully, the sun hammering relentlessly at their glistening, sweaty bodies, they made their way to the crest of the ridge, topped out, and dropped over to the yonder side. Shawn waited until the last bowed figure had disappeared, threw a long, searching glance to the trail up which the party had come to be certain there were no more, and then sighed heavily. He had almost blundered into the braves. If he hadn't turned off, headed for a knoll from which he intended to have a look at the surrounding country, he would have.

Mopping the sweat from his face and neck, he swung to the saddle, wincing as his backside came in contact with the sun-scorched leather. Roweling the big horse lightly, he rode up out of the pocket behind the rock, gained the summit of the hill for which he had been pointing, and shading his eyes, looked around.

He swore softly as his gaze swept over the shimmering, heat-blasted hell. He'd as well admit it — he was lost.

8

Not that he didn't know where he was — generally; deep in that seared, desolate land north of the Mexican border, which now lay miles to his right on the far side of the Rio Grande. . . . He was aware of that much, and it was of no help. Mexico was the last place he wanted to go at that moment.

His hoped for destination was the Hash Knife Ranch owned by a man named Hagerman. It was in the Carazones Peaks country. That was the rub; where the hell was the Carazones Peaks country? He had no sure idea of its location, and there was no one within miles — save that band of blooded braves — who could head him into the right direction, and he wasn't about to ask them.

There were peaks at about every point of the compass, smudgy, indefinite looking through the layers of dancing heat, and the map he'd scrawled into his mind back at Fort Davis didn't seem to fit in anywhere.

All he could say was that he was in deep, southwest Texas — a vast, formidable world of glittering rock, pitiless heat, starved cactus, withered shrubs, and little else. There were no roads, no definite trails — only untracked flats and slopes and vague, unreal formations lying dead under a blinding, steel sky. The Hash Knife Ranch could be anywhere.

He had hoped to reach Hagerman's the day before and by that high-noon hour have satisfied his reason for going there — that one of

9

Hash Knife's riders was or was not his brother Ben for whom he'd been searching so long.

The tip that such was a possibility had come to him in El Paso. He'd gone there after first journeying to Fort Worth and investigating a clue turned up in the small New Mexico town of Las Cruces. It, like all the others he'd pursued with such faithful persistence in the past, had proved false. Then, a stagecoach driver, in answer to the inquiries he routinely made wherever he happened to be, mentioned a passenger he had carried.

The description Shawn gave was a necessarily meager one as it had been well over ten years since Ben, in a burst of temper, had rebelled against the iron-fisted ways of their father, Hiram, and run away from their farm home in Ohio. But the driver felt his passenger fit and suggested that if Starbuck didn't mind the long, hot ride to the Carazones Peaks, it might prove worth his while.

Old Hiram Starbuck, in his will, had made the provision that before the estate could be settled equally between his two sons, Shawn, the younger, must find his errant brother. Until such was accomplished the thirty-thousand-dollar residue lying in the bank could not be touched — not even for expense money needed by Shawn to finance his quest.

In the beginning it had been a different and welcome change for him, still several years short of legal manhood. He had ridden away from his boyhood home filled with high hopes and the firm conviction that he would encounter no great difficulty in finding Ben and returning him to Ohio.

The months that followed proved otherwise. The small amount of cash the family lawyer had seen fit to advance him on his own initiative soon played out. Shawn was compelled to take a job, work for a time, and rebuild his capital in order to continue the search.

The pattern was thus established, and steadily and surely through the tedious days that followed, the farm boy who had never ventured more than a mile or two from the fieldstone house on the Muskingum River, changed into a tall, cool-eyed trail rider far older than his years, and one quick of mind and hand — a man others hoped would side with but never stand against them. . . .

Pulling off his hat, he forearmed the sweat from his face, stared moodily across the baked ground through eyelids narrowed to cut the intense glare. Reason told him the Carazones Peaks would lie to the east — but would he find them due east, or considerably to the south? He swore feelingly. In this empty sameness a man couldn't tell much about anything. It sure wasn't a country to go wandering aimlessly about — no towns, no ranches, no living persons, only transient Indians. It was a world abandoned to the cruelest, immoderate elements.

He could always turn around, head back north. There were a few small settlements that way, he thought, but he wasn't absolutely sure. He reckoned Fort Davis was his best bet if he decided to double back, but he disliked the thought of doing that after coming this far. If he did, he'd just have to swing back again as soon as he got his bearings. There ought to be some other answer.

One thing certain, he'd have to do something. Trail supplies were low and while he still had one full canteen of water, it wouldn't last indefinitely if he continued wandering about in this blistered slice of hell. He swore again, once more mopped at his face. The damned heat must be a hundred and ten or more.

Lazily, he came off the saddle, feeling the burn of the horn as he hooked his hand about it, and swung down. He grunted as his heels hit the solidness of the butte's crest, and immediately he felt the fire of the castigated soil spearing through the soles of his boots.

Ground reining the sorrel, he walked slowly to the edge of the formation. Off a few paces to his right a long-eared jackrabbit watched him indifferently from the filagreed shade of a snakeweed clump. No other living thing was to be seen; no birds overhead, no companion varmints to the jack — only the long-reaching, burning plains and hills and ghostlike peaks scattered helter-skelter in the distance as if the Power, in a moment of frivolity, had flung a handful of pinnacles across the scorched, level surface to relieve the monotony.

Shading his brow with a hand, he scoured the country with a painstaking probe, pivoting slowly to encompass a full three hundred and sixty degrees. At northeast he paused, interest whipping suddenly through him. . . . Smoke. . . . Or was it a dust devil whirling its wild way across the desert?

He brushed at the moisture beading his lashes, squinted hard. It wasn't dust. The thin banner twisting vertically upward was dark, not tan or yellow. He lowered his head, blinking to ease his aching eyes. . . . Smoke meant fire — and fire indicated a ranch or a town. It could also mean an Indian village, he thought wearily, or possibly a grass fire. The grama was dry enough to burst into flame of its own accord. But it was a streamer and that would tend to rule out a range fire.

He resumed his contemplation of the smoke. It now appeared to be growing thicker, and not dissipating. . . . A ranch or a town — it had to be one or the other. Hope lifted higher within him. The source of the twisting column was on the far side of a distant bank of hills, near the base of a soaring peak. It looked to be an area lying in the hollow of several high formations.

No matter, it was his one chance — and the only solution. He'd go there, which would actually amount to doubling back over his own tracks to some extent, except that he would be farther east, replenish his grub and water, and find out how to reach the Carazones Peaks. It would cost him at least a day, perhaps two, but it beat riding all the way back to Fort Davis or just wandering aimlessly about and ending up nowhere.

Coming around, his movements slow, utterly restricted by the driving heat, he returned to the gelding, stepped to the saddle, remembering this time to ease himself into the stove-hot leather hull gently, bit by bit. Finally settled, he threw another look to the wisping smoke, established its location with reference to several prominent landmarks, and rode down off the bluff.

Hours later, with endless miles of nothing but glittering sand, cat's-claw, saltbush, snakeweed, and cactus behind him in a glowing pit of invisible flame, he topped out a low ridge and looked down into a wide, shallow wash. A thin band of gray-green lay along its opposite bank, and relief stirred through him as his eyes caught the faint sparkle of silver — a creek.

The sorrel picked up the smell of the water at once, tossed his long head anxiously. Shawn let him move off immediately, dropping down onto the sandy floor and crossing at an eager walk until they came finally to the stream.

It was barely a trickle, but there was shade provided by a stand of stunted trees and a thin-leafed shrub unfamiliar to Starbuck. He halted at the creek's edge, climbed off, and with his foot, scraped out a hollow that filled slowly. Leaving it for the gelding, he unhooked his canteen, and while the horse sucked noisily at the small pool, had a swallow of the tepid water in the container.

The smoke was due north. The streamer seemed larger, darker now, but he guessed it was only because he was nearer. The presence of the creek cheered him, added credence to the belief there was a settlement or a ranch in the offing. Water was a scarce commodity — meant life in this desert world that seldom felt the kiss of raindrops, and the availability of the precious liquid in whatever quantity was a sure-fire guarantee that somewhere nearby humanity would be found.

A quarter hour later he was again in the saddle, refreshed somewhat by the brief inter-lude in the comparative coolness along the stream and by the feeling that his problem would soon find a solution. One thing was cer-tain, he'd do his traveling at night and during the early mornings from now on. A man was a damned fool to punish himself and his horse by moving about under that sun.

Looking ahead he could see the arroyo in which the creek flowed and that he was fol-lowing, was narrowing sharply and graduated into a steep-walled canyon. Abruptly he slowed as something else caught his attention. A short distance in front of him he saw the deep-cut ruts of wagon wheels crossing the stream at right angles. And then a bit farther on there were the hoofprints of cattle, a small herd, running parallel with the ruts as they also forded the stream. All ran east, aiming for a gap in the irregular horizon.

It would be a ranch, not a town, Starbuck concluded as he continued on. The cattle tracks were old, likely several weeks. The rancher would have been making a drive to market — a long journey from that location. He would be forced to take them east to where he'd hit the old Western Trail, as many called it, then swing north along its course to a final halt in Dodge City. . . . A long, hard drive. . . .

Starbuck, eyes on the breech in the skyline, felt the sorrel hesitate in stride. He looked around quickly. A frown pulled at his features. There no longer was a creek or a path skirting it; both had disappeared at the base of a towering rockslide.

☆ 2 ☆

Puzzled, Starbuck considered the vertical slab of granite. The stream simply went underground at this point; he understood that — but what had become of the path? Wheeling the sorrel, he backtracked to where the cattle and wagon had crossed, swung onto their trace. Urging the reluctant gelding with his spurs, Shawn headed him into the dense brush that lay west of the creek.

Staying on the ruts left by the broad, iron-tired wheels, he guided the sorrel through the tough growth. The vehicle had moved on no regular course, had simply carved a way through the sage and sand willow, straddling the clumps, forcing a passage that left little mark. A dozen yards farther on the prints veered from direct west to north. Starbuck kept the horse in one of the now faint tracks, realizing shortly that he was circling the rock formation.

Again the gelding slowed his step. A ragged wall of tall weeds, brush, and scattered rock once more blocked his way. Starbuck swore irritably. What the hell was it all about? He leaned forward, easing his aching muscles, eyes

17

on the tangled growth. There was something not exactly right about the brush — something unnatural. It came to him what it was — the brush was neatly interlaced. Here and there he could see small bits of rawhide string beneath the gray leaves.

Dismounting, he stepped up close to the wall. It was an improvised gate. Grasping it near what looked to be center, he puffed. The entire section came back with a dry rattling sound, disclosing an entrance into a short canyon. He could see the wagon-wheel ruts again along with the hoofprints of the passing cattle.

Lifting his gaze, he threw it beyond the narrow cleft. Far ahead lay a sprawling valley, green with grass and shaded with trees.

Shawn scrubbed at his jaw thoughtfully. Someone was taking great pains to keep the valley's location a secret, that was sure. On casual observation a passerby would think the wagon and the cattle came from somewhere to the west, had simply forded the creek at that point. Had he not been following the path along the stream it was likely he would have drawn the same conclusion.

Turned silent, he stood motionless in deep concentration — a tall, serious boy who became a man too early. In repose the leather-brown skin of his face was still smooth, showed only traces of fine lines at the corners of his eyes, blue now but cold gray in certain light.

18

He had but a thin beard and his hair was dark, and when somewhat long, as it was now, inclined to curl along his neck.

There was a confidence and an ever ready alertness to Shawn Starbuck that marked him as one who had ridden the uncounted miles of many trails and encountered all that accident and design had thrown at him — and survived. The mark of such was upon him, definite, and was there for all to see — and heed.

He'd not be welcome at that ranch, or whatever lay at the upper end of the distant valley. The brush-covered entrance made that a foregone truth. But he had no choice; he must have trail supplies and he needed information. He could not be on his way without both.

Reaching back he took up the sorrel's reins, led him through the gate, and pulled it back into place. Mounting, he continued, now on a well-defined trail.

The canyon broadened and the stream again was evident. More gentle growth became apparent and the stands of Christmas cholla, lechuguilla, and cat's-claw disappeared. Clusters of yellow-blossoming groundsel, clumps of jimson, white flowers folded against the sun, cluttered the receding slopes.

But shortly he saw he was coming to the end of the canyon. The valley, of which he'd been afforded but a small glimpse, lay farther still, somewhere beyond a hogback rising ahead.

He reached that level, halted, breath quickening at the sight of the wide, green expanse that stretched before him. That first look had surprised him, but he was totally unprepared for what he now saw. . . . Grass, trees in profusion, myriads of blue lupine, wild marigold and other flowers ablaze on all sides. The bright sparkle of not one but several streams met his gaze. . . . It was a scene wholly unexpected in the desolation across which he had come — and it was not difficult to understand why someone was most anxious to keep its location unknown.

But there was a strangeness to it all, a hushed restraint, a stillness that differed from that he felt on the flats where the very force of the remorseless sun and the vast emptiness of sheer space called down a coercing hush upon all things.

He became more conscious of the repressiveness as he pushed steadily toward the now more distinct column of smoke rising from beyond a second ridge near the valley's midway. When he finally gained the summit of that last roll and looked down upon a cluster of a dozen or so weathered shacks and buildings, he was even more aware of it.

It was a small settlement, he saw, and not a ranch. It appeared to be deserted, but the smoke rising from one of the structures belied that. Farther up the valley he could see farms lining each side, their plain, unpainted buildings squatting, bleak and forlorn, in the foreground. As near as he could tell the small plats of land, bountiful with fruit trees, corn standing tall and green, carpets of vegetables, extended the full length of the swale — twenty miles at least, possibly more.

Wiping at the sweat on his face, he urged the sorrel on, starting him down the easy grade at a brisk walk. Regardless of the welcome he might receive, it would be good to get off the saddle, wash up, have a meal cooked by hands other than his own. . . . And he'd sleep that night on a springs and mattress — give himself a treat.

That was a new thought, more than he had planned to do. He'd figured to just get supplies and directions and ride on. But the day was growing late. As well stay the night, start fresh in the morning while it was yet cool, make as far as he could before it got too hot, then pull up. He'd not lose much time.

He reached the outskirts of the village, again conscious of that strange restriction that seemed to hang over everything; it was as if he were entering some sort of void and it set up within him a faint disturbance. Once more he was struck by the abandoned appearance of it all. No living soul was in sight. Yet there were the rows of cultivated fields, the smoke winding up from a rock stack — the blacksmith shop, he noted — the curtained windows of the houses, a washing hanging on a line.

The first structures to his immediate right were vacant, the door of the second one sagging drunkenly from a single leather hinge, windows gaping open. To his left stood a livery barn, but he was unable to see into its dark recesses and could not tell if there was man or beast inside.

A general store, judging by what he could see behind the windows, was at the end of the dusty street; some distance back of it was a steepled church, its once whitewashed walls now a neglected gray. Close-by were several smaller houses and huts.

On the opposite side of the street from the store was what looked to be a feed and seed merchant. Next to him, and coming back up the narrow separation, was the blacksmith shop that had sent up its guiding plume of black for him to follow. Next to that lean-to building was the two-story bulk of what served as a hotel. Beyond and around these major structures were more smaller houses — residences, Starbuck assumed.

He drew up across from the hotel, a curious fact dawning on him; none of the business places bore names or any lettered indication as to the nature of the establishment. It was as if the owners did not wish their identities known, nor care to divulge the nature of the trade they were engaged in.

Evidently it was up to any possible customer to ferret out the source for his needs. . . . That would be the case, Shawn reflected, where a stranger was concerned — and because no strangers ever visited the hidden valley with its bleak settlement, it posed no problem.

He dismounted slowly, digesting this all as his eyes covered the street, the windows of the buildings and houses, the doors that stood open in most instances to gather in any vagrant, cooling breeze.

No one had appeared — no man, no woman, no child. Not even a dog contested his arrival — an event that one could ordinarily expect to encounter upon riding into a town. Somewhere he could hear chickens clucking, and that homey sound did something to break the tension that, unknowingly, had built within him.

There were people — somewhere. They were simply avoiding him, keeping out of sight, afraid for one reason or another to make their presence known.

Why? Did it have to do with the carefully hidden entrance to the valley? He shrugged. There was a reason, a good one, no doubt — but it didn't concern him. Come daylight he'd be on his way, leaving them to their secret paradise.

Walking stiffly, bathed in sweat, he crossed the street to the hitchrack fronting what he was assuming to be a hotel. Winding the sorrel's leathers around the bar, he took his saddlebags and rifle, mounted the two steps to the porch. Pausing there for one more look up and down the street, he entered the open doorway.

23

☆ 3 ☆

The lobby was fairly large. It was stuffy with motionless, heated air; and light, entering through the doorway and a single window fronting on the street, only partly relieved the gray shadows streaking the area.

A bench and a few straight-backed chairs stood against the walls. A long, narrow table built from rough lumber was near the center and supplied surface for several yellowing almanacs.

Opposite the entrance a counter arrangement had been constructed. Half a dozen pegs, with keys dangling on rawhide string, protruded from a whitewashed board that was affixed prominently to the wall behind the improvised desk. It was as if the management wished to convey the impression that privacy was available on the premises — if little else.

Still conscious of the disturbing, eerie quiet, and wondering at the absence of life, Shawn crossed to the counter. There was no tap bell on the dusty board, and after a few moments he rapped sharply.

A door at the end of the lobby opened. A balding, cadaverous man, with the left sleeve of his butternut shirt hanging empty, reluctantly entered, made his way in behind the counter. He had small, dark eyes that peered out from beneath a shelf of ragged, graying brows in which Starbuck could read suspicion and mistrust.

"Need a room," Shawn said.

The man glanced beyond him to the street. "You alone?"

"I'm alone."

The hotel man frowned as if disbelieving. "You looking for somebody then — maybe figuring to meet them here?"

Sweaty, worn from the long hot day, hungry, Starbuck stirred impatiently. "No, I'm not looking for anybody. I'm by myself — and I don't expect to meet somebody. All I'm after is a good meal and a room for the night. Can you oblige me, or not?"

The man's shoulders lost some of their tense rigidity. Reaching back he took one of the keys from its peg, laid it on the counter.

"Room at the head of the stairs. I'll see you get some fresh water."

Shawn picked up the key. "There a stable out back? Horse of mine needs —"

"I'll see to him."

"He's the sorrel," Starbuck said, and then shrugged. There was no necessity for being so specific; the gelding was the only horse on the street. He turned for the stairs, paused, curiosity piquing him. "Town's deserted, seems. Something wrong?"

The clerk's face blanked, his eyes became expressionless. "Oh, folks are around somewheres," he said vaguely, and then manner changing, he came out from behind the counter. Extending his hand, he said, "Name's Simon Pierce. Yours?"

"Starbuck — Shawn Starbuck."

"Glad to meet you, Starbuck. Shawn. . . . That got something to do with the Indians?"

"Shawnee tribe. My ma took the name from that."

"What I figured. . . . Just passing through?"

"Be riding on in the morning. Want pay for the room now?"

Pierce wagged his head. "Morning'll be fine. Can settle up for the horse, too."

"You want me to register then?"

"Register? Oh — well, I don't keep no regular book like that. No need for it around here. Just forget it."

Starbuck hung the saddlebags over his shoulder, grasped the rifle by its action, moved for the steps. Again he hesitated, looked to Pierce, now heading for the front door.

"Soon as I put this gear in my room and wash up, I'll be wanting a meal. There a place to eat?"

Once more a stilled, thoughtful expression claimed the one-armed man's features. A strong flow of doubt seemed to tear at him, possess him, and then he shrugged as if dismissing it all.

"Ain't no restaurant, but we've got what you'd call a dining room." He pointed to a door at the south end of the lobby. "In there. The wife and daughter'll take care of you."

The room was dark, choked with stale trapped air. Shawn tossed the leather pouches onto the bed, stood the rifle in a corner, and thinking of Pierce's strange actions, crossed to the single window. Throwing up the oilcloth shade, he drew back, absently watched the fine dust filter down onto the sill in a filmy sheet.

The hotel enjoyed few patrons, it was clear. He doubted the room had been occupied in months; and from the reaction of the townspeople to his arrival, it appeared they hadn't seen a stranger in years! Such was possible, he had to admit as he tugged at the window in an effort to loosen it in its frame, considering the hidden entrance to the valley.

There was a knock at the door, and propping the window open with a short length of wood provided for the purpose, he crossed the room and drew back the panel. No one was there but a bucket of water was waiting for him. Picking it up, he filled the china pitcher, poured the remainder into the companion bowl.

Washing his face and neck, hands and arms, he dried himself with the threadbare towel hanging from a hook above the washstand. . . . Later he'd strip, clean himself properly because there didn't seem to be much hope of getting a real bath in a tub at a barber shop.

Fact of the matter was, he hadn't noticed a barber along the street. He scratched at his jaw; there were quite a few odd things about the town — whatever its name was.

Pulling on his shirt, he hitched at the low slung forty-five hanging on his left hip, and leaving the room, descended to the lobby. There was no sign of Pierce, and walking to the front door, he glanced out. The sorrel was gone. He grunted in satisfaction at that. The big red horse needed looking after. He'd had a hard day. Wheeling, he recrossed the lobby to the door Simon had indicated, opened it, and entered.

He paused just inside. The room, smaller than the lobby and at the rear of the building, had four or five tables with accompanying quartets of chairs placed here and there. Three roughly dressed, hard-looking men occupied a corner position. All looked up at his entrance, studied him with calculating coldness.

A bottle of whiskey was on the table before them, and this, too, brought a realization to Shawn; there had been no saloons on the street either.

Briefly nodding to the trio, he turned to the opposite corner, sat down back to the wall so that he faced the entire room. It was a subconscious habit, one acquired possibly as a need always to be aware of his surroundings and of those who moved about him. It also satisfied a need to simply watch people and observe their ordinary actions. . . . A man riding an endless trail finds loneliness an ever present companion.

He felt the critical gaze of the hardcases still on him, and easing back in his chair, he returned their stare with unblinking assurance. At once all looked away. One, a dark man with a scruffy black beard and fish-cold gray eyes, reached for the bottle. The remnants of the meal they had just eaten were still before them.

The rider tipped the bottle to his lips, took a long pull. Immediately the man to his left, a thin, quiet individual with a scar tracing from the corner of an eye to the edge of his mouth, extended a hand for the liquor.

"All right, Abe, you don't have to hog it. Could save me and Bobby Joe a little."

Bobby Joe appeared to be the youngest of the three. He, too, was dark, but with a scanty growth of hair, and a way of nervously flipping his eyes about.

Shawn considered the men from hooded eyes. He wondered if they were local residents or if they, too, as had he, stumbled onto the hidden valley and its small settlement. Likely such was the truth. Somehow they didn't seem to belong. . . . A second thought came to Shawn; could they be the cause of the paralysis that gripped the town?

He shifted wearily, swung his glance to the wall to his right in which was the door that evidently led into the kitchen. Whatever — it was of no interest to him. He was there by accident, wished nothing but food, rest, and information as to how he could reach the Carazones Peaks country.

The kitchen door swung open. A girl, seventeen, possibly eighteen years of age, face flushed with heat, round, blue eyes bright, her lips set to a firm line, entered. Casting a sidelong glance at the three men in the corner, she started across the room for Starbuck.

This would be Simon Pierce's daughter, he guessed, and she was frightened. There was no doubt of that. He watched her approach, noting that she was pretty in a doll-like way, and had a neatly rounded figure that was not entirely concealed by the voluminous garment she wore.

As she passed the table where the men were, a laugh went up. Bobby Joe half rose, reached for her, saying something in a low voice. The girl jerked away, cheeks flushing, the shine of fear brightening in her eyes.

She came to a halt before Starbuck, glared down at him. "Well?"

He studied her, faintly amused by the anger she was directing at him, and then said, "Supper, if it's all right with you. Steak, potatoes — plenty of both — and whatever else is handy. Like some light bread, but biscuits will do. Pot of coffee. Can talk about pie later."

The girl bobbed her head. "If you're wanting whiskey, we don't have any."

"Never mix my eating with my drinking,"

Starbuck drawled. He swung his glance to the men. "They giving you trouble?"

"No more than I can handle," she snapped, but she plainly was reluctant to recross the room and return to the kitchen.

"Expect you can. You'd be Simon Pierce's daughter."

"Yes, I'm Hetty. Why?"

"No reason. Took a room for the night and he mentioned you and your ma ran the dining room. This town got a name?"

Hetty Pierce slid a sidelong glance at the corner table. Bobby Joe was still hunched forward on his chair watching, waiting. Abe and the scar-faced one were slumped in their seats, heads slung low as if dozing.

"No, I guess it really hasn't," Hetty said, coming back to Starbuck. "This is what folks call the Hebren Valley. I suppose you could call the town that, too — only it's not exactly a town."

"Was wondering about that."

"We call it a Community — we're sort of a sect. Everyone works together, like a family. Combine our labor and share equally the fruits — that's the way Oram Grey — he's our Senior Elder — likes to put it."

"Those aren't regular stores along the street?"

"No, sometimes we call them that but they're more like warehouses or storage depots. Everything we produce is put into them, and we all

31

draw what we need as time goes along."

Shawn nodded understandingly. He knew now why there were no names on the buildings, why there was so little activity.

"Noticed where a herd of cattle had been driven out. You raise beef, too?"

Hetty looked again at Bobby Joe. He still faced her, his hot, bold glance raking her continually.

"Some. The men — all the younger ones — drove our herd to market over a month ago and they're not back yet. First time we've ever sent cattle to market. We do more farming than anything else. How did you happen to come here?"

"Got myself lost looking for the Carazones Peaks country. Saw smoke and tracked it down. Was coming from your blacksmith shop. . . . Getting powerful hungry. You want me to walk you back to the kitchen?"

Hetty's lips tightened. "Never mind," she murmured, and turned away.

She walked straight at Bobby Joe and then, when almost upon him, veered suddenly, reached for a chair at an adjoining table. Sliding it toward him, she effectively blocked him off, and hurried on.

Bobby Joe's eyes flashed with anger, and then he laughed, slapped the top of the table. Settling back, he reached for the bottle, took a quick drink. The man with the scar stirred, looked up.

"What's biting you?"

"That there priss of a gal!" Bobby Joe replied, taking another swallow of the liquor. "Keeps waltzing me off."

The older man rubbed at his chin. "Was you smart, you'd leave her be —"

Bobby Joe snorted. "Rollie the big know-it-all about women! When'd you get to be so smart?"

"Long time ago — and I've seen her kind before. Once knew a cowpoke that took a fancy to a girl like her. Just kept warting her all the time but she plain wouldn't have nothing to do with him. Then one day she got real sweet like and baked him a mistletoe pie — only she told him it was a gooseberry. Well, she wasn't bothered none by him no more after that 'cause it killed him dead. . . . You keep messing around and something like that's going to happen to you."

"Not her. She's just honing for me to take her. Playing it cozy, that's all."

"Acts to me like she don't favor you none a'tall."

"That's because you don't know nothing about women. Anyway, whether she's willing or not, it ain't nobody's business but mine. . . . Didn't hear you hollering when Abe took on that yellow-haired gal he keeps meeting up with."

"Different. She's a growed woman and looking to be took. Plain she's been needing a buck young enough to do her some good for a long time, seeing as how she's got a husband more'n twicet her age. But this here Hetty, she's only a kid —"

"Kid — hell! And she's sure ready. Was watching her go to bed the other night and —"

"So that's where you was! Dammit, Bobby Joe, you cut out that tomfoolery — leastwise until Con gets here. Then if he says it's all right, then all right — but I ain't letting you mess things up until he does! Hear?"

"Sure, I'm hearing. . . . There ain't no chance of stirring up nothing."

"Hell there ain't!"

"You'll see. First thing you know I'll have her eating out of my hand like a little kitty cat. . . ."

Starbuck was listening idly. It sounded as if the men did belong in Hebren Valley, that Bobby Joe was endeavoring to make up to Hetty Pierce and was having no luck. But their words were harsh and they seemed not in character with the sort of persons he figured would populate the area. . . . Too, it had been fear he saw in Hetty's eyes — as well as those of Simon Pierce.

The kitchen door opened. Hetty, a platter heaped with food in one hand, a cup and saucer in the other, appeared, began to make her way warily toward Starbuck.

Bobby Joe came to his feet, a wicked grin on his lips. He lunged forward, caught the girl around the waist, and settled back onto his chair, drawing Hetty, precariously balancing the platter and the coffee, onto his lap.

"I think I'll just eat that there steak myself, honeybunch," he said, laughing. "And you can feed it to me, whilst I tell you what you and me are going to do —"

Starbuck, anger rising within him at the abuse the girl was being compelled to endure as well as seeing his supper snatched away from him, rose quickly. In two long strides he crossed to where Hetty struggled to free herself of Bobby Joe's strong, roving hands.

Snatching the platter from her, Shawn jerked the rider's stained hat down over his eyes, wedging it tight to the nose, and pulled the girl free. Wheeling, he started back for his table, hearing the enraged cursing of Bobby Joe, the surprised questions of Abe and Rollie, once again aroused from their stupor.

On beyond the entrance to the kitchen Shawn could see the strained, worried face of Simon Pierce, and next to him a thinner, older edition of Hetty, her features also taut with fear.

The truth of the situation dawned upon Starbuck in that instant as he caught the look in the eyes of Hetty's parents. Rollie, Bobby Joe, Abe — they weren't local residents, members of the Hebrenite sect; they were outsiders, outlaws undoubtedly, who had moved in, probably during the absence of the settlement's younger men who were away on the cattle drive.

That they had terrorized the people was evident by the very fact that all were remaining hidden, unseen. The Pierces, being the operators of the hotel and the only place where meals could be obtained, were bearing the brunt of their presence. Such was particularly true where Hetty was concerned.

Shawn sighed inwardly. Regardless of where he went there was always trouble of some sort. It was impossible it seemed, to move through life without encountering it and try as he would to not become involved, he always ended up in the entanglement.

This time it would be different. This time he was going to stay out of it, come blizzard, blasphemy, or the rebuilding of Babylon. He'd eat, go to bed, sleep, and in the morning get the grub and information he needed — and ride out. The sooner he could get to Hagerman's Hash Knife Ranch and find out if Ben — or he guessed he should call him Damon Friend because that was the name that he was going by in New Mexico — was there, the better. If need be he'd —

"Look out!"

☆ 4 ☆

At Hetty's shrill warning, Shawn pivoted. Bobby Joe crashed into him from the left side, jarred him solidly. The plate of food slipped from his hand, fell to the floor.

Biting back his anger, mindful of his determination to not become involved, Starbuck righted himself, fell back a half step.

"No need for this," he said. "Was my supper —"

"The hell you say!" Bobby Joe shouted, and rushed in once more.

Shawn sidestepped easily, and then abruptly furious, he caught the rider by the arm, swung him around. Off balance, staggering, Bobby Joe rocked forward. Starbuck's knotted fist caught him with a down-sledging blow to the jaw, drove him to his hands and knees.

Rollie yelled something. Shawn glanced up quickly. Bobby Joe's two friends were on their feet but showed no indication of participating, only of shouting advice and encouragement to their champion, now shaking his head in an effort to clear it.

Shawn drew back, almost slipping on the mess underfoot. Still simmering, he leaned over, clamped strong fingers on the back of Bobby Joe's neck, and with a sweep of his booted foot, kicked the man's supporting arms from beneath him.

Bobby Joe flopped forward. Starbuck, dragging him around, shoved his face into the scramble of meat, gravy and fried potatoes, ground it about thoroughly.

"You wanted my supper," he snapped. "Now eat it!"

Bobby Joe, choking and spluttering, yelled a smothered oath, fought to escape the inexorable pressure of Shawn's grip on his neck.

Finally satisfied, Starbuck released his hold, stepped back. His anger had cooled somewhat, and after a moment he drew a chair from an adjoining table, sat down, and motioned to Hetty.

"Be obliged if you'll bring me another order of the same."

The girl, wide-eyed, a frozen smile parting her lips, nodded woodenly. "Yes, sir," she murmured, and wheeling, hurried off into the kitchen, brushing by her stony-faced parents without a word.

Shawn slumped in his chair but at coiled-spring alert, watched Bobby Joe pull himself to his knees. Bits of potato clung to his thin beard and crumbs of mashed biscuit plastered his forehead and cheeks. Grease smeared over his face gave it a dull shine.

Twisting his head, he brought his burning

eyes to bear on Starbuck. Hate throbbed in their depths as he scraped the mess from his features with a cupped hand.

"Goddamn you — you son of a bitch!" he mouthed. "I'll kill you for that! I'll —"

Starbuck shrugged. "Get some help," he said indifferently.

Instantly, without rising, Bobby Joe threw himself at Shawn. Arms outflung, he encircled Starbuck's legs, and pushing hard with his feet, toppled man, chair, and all to the floor.

Starbuck kicked free as he crashed to the hard boards. Catlike, he rolled to his feet. He heard a sound behind him, jerked to one side, took the butt of Abe's pistol aimed at his head, on a shoulder. Spinning, he drove a rock-hard right fist into the older man's belly, sent him stumbling and retching for breath back into his chair. Instantly he wheeled to face Bobby Joe surging in.

The young outlaw staggered him with a good, roundhouse right to the jaw. Subconsciously, he dropped back two steps, fell into the cocked stance of a trained boxer — just as he'd been taught to do by his father.

Be smart. You get hurt, throw up your guard, and stall — give your head time to clear. That was what old Hiram, who had received his training from an English champion, had told him. And Hiram Starbuck knew well the art; while never boxing professionally, he had prided himself on the weekly exhibition matches he had put on in the town near their Ohio farm.

So proficient was Hiram and so appreciative his admirers that they one day presented him with an ornately decorated silver belt buckle upon which was imposed the ivory figure of a boxer in the familiar fist-raised stance of the expert. It was now one of Shawn's prized possessions and worn constantly by him.

"Well, hi-di-hi!" Rollie yelled from the table as Bobby Joe paused. "Would you look at what we got here!"

Starbuck continued to circle, backing carefully, allowing his faculties to return to normal, maintaining a close watch on his rear to be certain no one would slip in behind him again.

"One of them fancy-dan fighters we been hearing about!" Bobby Joe shouted, taking up the derision. He was making a great show of it, projecting it not only to his companions but also to the Pierces gathered in the doorway of the kitchen.

"Here's where I show you folks how a real fighting man does a job — and does it without all that running and dancing!"

Shawn considered the outlaw with taut amusement. His head had cleared entirely and he awaited only an opening to step in, finish off Bobby Joe and have done with it. Abe and Rollie had pulled back seemingly confident now that their partner could take care of himself.

Abruptly Bobby Joe pushed in, fists swinging.

Shawn feinted neatly, crossed with a slashing left that brought quick blood to the corner of the man's mouth, followed with a right that smacked solidly into the side of the head.

Bobby Joe yelled, halted flat-footed. He shook himself as if in disbelief. He hadn't touched Starbuck, yet had taken two shocking blows. Wheeling, he swore loudly, came in fast.

Once more Shawn, shifting like a fleeting shadow in sunlight, moved in, smashed a combination left and right to Bobby Joe's face, again danced away. The young outlaw bellowed his frustration, spun, threw himself at Starbuck. Shawn, taking several wild, aimless blows that did no harm, ducked low, began hammering the man mercilessly about the head, the belly, and the ribs. He kept at it for several seconds, driving like the pistons of a locomotive. Bobby Joe began to wilt. Shawn moved lightly away.

Wiping at the sweat clothing his face, sucking for wind, he watched the outlaw narrowly. The man's knees were trembling, seemed hardly able to support him. He'd had about enough. Slowly then Bobby Joe sank to hands and knees. His head came forward, hair stringing down over his glazed eyes. Rollie was yelling at him to get up, to show the fancy dan a thing or two — to fight.

Bobby Joe seemed not to hear. He remained motionless. Shawn moved forward. Raising a leg, he placed his foot against the outlaw's shoulder, shoved hard. Bobby Joe went over sideways onto his back, arms and legs outflung.

Rollie cursed, came in fast. Starbuck, not expecting the charge, attempted to sidestep, slipped on the grease-smeared floor, half fell. He took a sharp blow to the ear from the scar-faced man, another high on the head.

He winced as Rollie drove the toe of a boot into his belly. Pain roared through him as a second kick found his groin. Buckling, he pivoted away, felt the outlaw's weight come down upon him as the man threw himself upon his back, looped an arm around his neck.

Furious, struggling to keep his footing, Starbuck finally got himself firmly stanched. Reaching up he grasped Rollie's forearm, locked tight against his windpipe, tore it loose. Bending in a quick, humping motion, he swung his weight forward, threw his strength into his hands. Rollie went soaring over his head, crashed into the nearby wall.

A clattering of dishes sounded as shelves on the opposite side of the partition spilled their loads. Shawn, thoroughly aroused, wheeled to face Abe, saw the outlaw, gun in hand, rising from his chair.

The outlaw's features still had a pasty color, effects of the blow he'd taken, but there was a hard, murderous glint in his eyes. Shawn's hand swept down for the holster on his hip. Alarm rocked him. The forty-five was not there. He'd lost it sometime during the scuffle. He looked hurriedly about, spotted the weapon under the table to his left — two long strides away.

"Don't try it!" Abe muttered.

In that same instant Shawn heard Hetty shout, saw motion from the corner of his eye as she threw the cup and saucer she held straight at the man. Instantly he lunged for his pistol, snatched it up, and rolled away, upending the table, sending several chairs skittering across the floor.

Flat on his belly, forty-five leveled, he faced Abe. The rider, pistol hanging at his side, was mopping coffee from his eyes with a forearm. Rising slowly, he nodded at the man coldly.

"Put that iron away — unless you figure to use it."

Silent, Abe slid the weapon back into its holster. Starbuck waggled the barrel of his pistol at Bobby Joe, now struggling to his feet, and then at the scarred Rollie, who lay motionless against the base of the wall.

"Get 'em out of here —"

☆ 5 ☆

Abe turned reluctantly, knelt beside Rollie, and shook the man to half consciousness. Rising, he beckoned to Bobby Joe for assistance.

Somewhat unsteady the younger rider crossed to where his friend had pulled the scarfaced Rollie to a sitting position, and draping one of the man's limp arms about his neck, assumed a share of the burden. Together they got him upright and started for the door.

Hetty barred their way. "I'll have a dollar pay from each of you," she said, eyes flashing. "This is one meal you're paying for!"

The outlaws came to a halt. Abe groaned, glanced to Bobby Joe. The young outlaw's lips drew back into a sneer.

"The hell you say! We ain't paying for —"

"You are this time — and from now on, else you stay out!"

Bobby Joe stared at her, shook his head. "Go to the devil," he said, and nodding to Abe, resumed the slow march for the lobby door.

Shawn, hand resting on the butt of his holstered weapon, moved toward them. "You heard the lady. Pay up."

Again the three men came to a stop. Bobby

Joe's face was taut, and his dark eyes glittered as he swung them to Starbuck.

"Mister, you're sure bucking for the grave-yard!"

"Maybe," Shawn replied quietly. "Meantime, you'll pay what you owe."

Abe shrugged, dug into his pocket with a free hand, and produced several coins. Dropping three silver dollars on the table beside him, he touched Starbuck with a hating glance, and then again the outlaws moved on.

Silent, fingers still hooked lightly about the handle of his pistol, Shawn watched the men pass through the doorway into the dark lobby. He did not stir until he had seen their dark silhouettes block briefly the street entrance to the hotel and then disappear into the open. Only then did he turn and resume his seat at the table.

"Like that meal now," he said tiredly to Hetty and her parents, standing quietly to one side.

He was beat, hungry, and uncomfortable from the dried sweat plastering his body. He ached dully in several places from the blows delivered by Bobby Joe and Rollie, and there was a stinging along his jaw where a ring one of the outlaws was wearing had etched a deep scratch.

What the hell was wrong with him? Was he trouble prone — as some people seemed to be accident prone? What sort of freak luck forever attended him, drew him into someone else's problems? For once — just once — he'd like to be left alone to go about his business and —

"Mr. Starbuck — reckon I ought to thank you."

It was *Mr. Starbuck* now, Shawn noticed as Simon Pierce's voice cut into his thoughts. The art of courtesy drilled into him by his schoolteacher mother and the need to employ it when dealing with others, regardless of circumstances, pushed the sardonic irritation from him.

"No need," he murmured, not missing the thread of disfavor in the tone of the one-armed man — and misinterpreting it. "Whatever the damage is, add it to my bill."

He fell silent again, watched Hetty gather up the silver dollars, move toward her father, hand extended.

"Damage won't amount to anything," she said, catching the last of his words. Her eyes still glowed from the excitement. "Worth it anyway. It's the first time they've been taken down since they rode in here — weeks ago!"

Simon Pierce cupped the silver coins in his hand, studied them with no expression. "Sorry this had to happen. . . . Afraid it'll mean more trouble for you."

Starbuck smiled wryly. Through the kitchen doorway he could see Mrs. Pierce busy at the stove. The smell of frying potatoes and sizzling steak wafted to him, further whetting his appetite.

"I'll hear from them — no doubt of that.

Their kind never let things lie. Have to get in their licks, somehow. . . . But it's nothing to fret over. Who are they?"

"Outlaws — army deserters. There's more of them coming here. They're hanging around, waiting for them."

"This a regular thing?"

"No, first time for these three. Seems Kilrain — he's one of them they're waiting for — was here during the war. Army patrol or something. They stumbled onto the valley by accident."

Shawn nodded absently. "Same as I did."

"Reckon so. Name of Kilrain's sort of familiar. May recognize him when I see him again. He's the head of a gang of outlaws. He decided our valley, being hid away like it is, would make a fine hideout. Going to use it for their headquarters. The three that you run into tonight came on ahead, are waiting for him and the rest to show up. . . . Leastwise, that's the way we figure it from what they've told us and the scraps of talk we've picked up."

"Sounds like you don't want them around. Why don't you run them out?"

"With what — and who?" Hetty demanded in a bitter voice before her father could speak.

Simon Pierce frowned, glanced to his daughter reprovingly. "Never mind, girl. . . . What she means is, there's not a weapon among us — in the whole valley, unless you want to call axes and tools like that, weapons. You see, we don't believe in violence."

"And if we had guns there's nobody around to use them," Hetty added. "Every man able to ride a horse — even the larger boys — are on the cattle drive. We couldn't run them off even if we had the means."

Starbuck shifted on his chair. "When the others return, you can straighten it all out."

"Likely," Simon Pierce said, "but that won't be for a couple more weeks, maybe longer."

"And by then," Hetty finished, "those cutthroats will have settled in good and we'll never be rid of them! They'll own the valley and everyone and everything in it."

"Looks like you'd best change some of your thinking," Shawn said, glancing hopefully toward the kitchen where Mrs. Pierce was removing a pan from the oven of the stove. "Hardcases like Bobby Joe and his pals only understand force. You can't go easy on them or they'll run you right into the ground."

"We've been folks who've lived without violence for generations," Pierce said slowly. "And we've survived, even those who set themselves against us and oppressed us. Expect we can do so again where Kilrain and his gang are concerned."

"Generations?" Starbuck repeated. "You been here that long?"

"Not exactly right here all that time. Our Family, as we call it, got started in Pennsylvania about a hundred years ago."

"Probably would've been smart to stay there.

Better chance for your way of living than here where a man has to depend pretty much on a gun."

"It wasn't exactly a single group then — just several different families all living in one part of the country. Floods hit every summer, Indian troubles, now and then droughts — always something that kept wiping them out.

"Was a man by the name of Hebren — Malachi Hebren who was sort of the leader. One day he got the idea of them all banding together, throwing what they owned into one basket, so to speak, and then pooling their labor so as to stand up against misfortune as a single party instead of as individuals. Thus, sharing, nobody would ever want. Idea worked, and later on they got to calling it Hebren's Family, and those who were in it — my folks at that time — Hebrenites.

"Family soon got pretty big and some of them moved to Missouri, but that state got all torn up by the talk of war, some folks being for the Union, some siding with the South. Came down to where a man had to decide where he stood and declare himself.

"That's when we picked up and moved out. Hetty was just a little one then, two, three years old. Leader of our Family, the Senior Elder he's called, was and still is Oram Grey. He'd heard of this country and about this valley. Didn't know exactly where it was, and we spent the best part of a year hunting it, but we finally come across it, moved in and settled down to living the way we figure folks ought to live — at peace with each other."

"We can't look at it that way any longer, papa," Hetty said impatiently. "They've spoiled it — these outlaws — and we're either going to have to fight them or pick up and move on again — just like the Family did in Missouri and Illinois and Pennsylvania, and all the other places where we've been set upon and hounded into leaving."

Simon Pierce nodded sadly. "If we have to move on, that's what we'll do. Be hard this time, however. This here's a beautiful valley and it's been mighty good to us. We've prospered — crops, cattle, our people —"

"What's left of them," Hetty said scornfully. "The young ones, leastwise the boys, run off as soon as they're big enough. . . . I would, too, if I could."

"Hush, girl," Pierce said. "Your day will come, your time to marry, have your own —"

"My time's come and gone! There's no men left my age that I can take as a husband. They've all gone, and there's only old Ezrah Vinsent and —"

"Hush!" Pierce said again, more sternly. "Time will take care of your needs, and you will be provided for."

"Not with a husband — that's for sure! Youngest unmarried man in the Family now is Ezrah and he's near seventy. The oldest boy is thirteen. . . . What kind of a choice is that?"

"Time will provide," Pierce insisted doggedly. "Problems are solved by patience and understanding. Always have been. Yours will be also."

"Maybe, but before all the younger men weren't leaving as soon as they were big enough."

Starbuck, weary of the bickering that had nothing to do with him, looked again to the kitchen. The Hebrenites and Hetty had trouble, but there was nothing he could do to help them. And as Simon Pierce had said, matters had worked themselves out in the past, likely they would do so in the future. One thing did stir interest within him, however.

"How've you managed to keep this place a secret all these years? Know you keep the trail blocked and the entrance hidden, but expect you have to send out now and then for some supplies, things you can't make or grow, like coffee."

"Mostly we get along without the things we can't provide, but you're right, there are a few items we must buy in the outside world. . . . Window glass, iron, a few other things. Oram Grey sees to it, and only those appointed by him are permitted to leave the valley for such purposes."

"It's — it's like a prison," Hetty murmured, biting at her lower lip. "A terrible prison!"

"We have two men who do what freighting is necessary," Pierce continued, ignoring the girl. "And the cattle drive — our first — is led by

51

Tolliver Grey, Oram's son. The men and the boys with him, and the freighters, will never speak of the valley. It is bred into them — and they know the value of secrecy. Nobody will ever learn of the place from them."

"Those outlaws found it."

"An accident, Kilrain's coming here. Those are the things we can not protect ourselves against — and it may cause us to move once more."

"Was that army patrol the first to stumble onto your valley in all the years that you've been here?"

"The first and last until Bobby Joe and Abe and Rollie rode in — and you, of course. Their coming was no accident. Kilrain told them how to find it."

Shawn could understand why the valley had gone unnoticed. The surrounding country, wild, desolate, and heat ravaged, extended no invitation to travelers. To the contrary, likely all avoided it as they would the plague.

"It'll make a good hideout for Kilrain and his bunch," Shawn commented. "You won't find any posses wanting to hunt the country around here for them. Might call your valley an outlaw's heaven."

"Especially when they'll have the whole town waiting on them hand and foot, looking after their needs even when it comes to women like Esther Grey —"

"Hetty!"

The sharpness in Simon Pierce's voice stilled

52

the girl's tongue for the first time. Suddenly downcast, she turned away.

"I'll see if your supper isn't about ready," she murmured to Shawn, and moved off toward the kitchen.

Pierce watched her go, shook his head. "Sometimes I think being young is the hardest time of life. There's so much to do, but so little permitted. I'm often sorry for them."

"She's right about one thing," Starbuck said. "Sure no business of mine, but you won't be able to keep your young people much longer under your thumb, the way you have. Losing them already, in fact. Know I'd find it hard to stay cooped up in one place all my life, no matter how fine everything was."

"Even if you had no worries about where your meals would come from, where you would sleep, or how you would get clothes to put on your back or boots on your feet? We have our own schoolteachers who work from the best books we're able to get. Our women — all of them — are expert in medicine, better than many doctors, and can handle any problem. Every need of our people is cared for.

"In the world outside, a man's got to have money to live and to support his family with. In our Community there is no such thing as want — or worry over it. The Family shares equally all that is possessed. Nobody has any need for money, just as nobody ever suffers or goes without."

Shawn leaned back. He could see Hetty dishing up his food, heaping a platter high.

"Don't think your way's exactly new," he said. "Indians've been doing it that way, more or less, for a long time."

"And you don't agree that it's good — better than the hard scramble to stay alive that outsiders have to face?"

"Can't agree to anything that keeps a man tied down against his will. If he likes your way — fine. It's his life, his business. But I can't see penning him or any of your folks here unless they want it that way."

"You were raised different, taught the kind of life most people face — slaving to make a living, sometimes starving and suffering and never knowing the quiet, peaceful paths that men are supposed to enjoy. . . . The sort of life you speak of is a struggle — one where a man is actually at war with another in his fight to provide for himself and those who depend upon him."

"Which, to my way of thinking is how it ought to be," Shawn replied. "Man should stand on his own two feet, rely on himself and nobody else."

"The old way," Pierce said wearily. "It's not the right one simply because it was what you were taught, what others you know do. . . . That it is what others have always done don't make it right."

Hetty emerged from the kitchen bringing the

platter — well filled as before with meat, potatoes, string beans, and thin slices of onion — in one hand. In the other she carried a tin of biscuits smeared with honey.

Brushing aside her father, she set the food on the table in front of Shawn and moved away, making room for her mother.

"My wife, Patience," Simon said, remembering no introduction had been made.

The older woman nodded to Starbuck, waved him back into his chair as he half rose to acknowledge her.

"I'm thanking you for what you done — whether the men folk like it or not," she said smilingly. "And this is my own special way," she added, placing a saucer with a thick wedge of hot apple pie capped with melting butter near his plate. "Hetty, bring the coffee."

The girl turned away at once. Patience, bulky in her Mother Hubbard garment, swung about to face her husband.

"And Simon, you've done nothing but nigh talk Mr. Starbuck to death. Now you can do something good for him. He'll be wanting a bath soon's he's finished with his vittles. You get yourself busy and lug the tub and some buckets of water up to his room. Hear?"

☆ 6 ☆

Shawn grinned his approval of Patience's crisp words, glanced at the appetizing food, and rose.

"Something wrong?" Hetty asked anxiously.

Starbuck moved for the door and into the lobby. "Figured I'd best have a look, be sure I'm not about to have visitors. Like to eat this meal in peace."

The girl followed to the entrance of the hotel. A few persons were now in the street, conversing, casting glances furtively in their direction. Others were coming. Looking around Shawn could see no signs of the outlaws.

"Bobby Joe — and the others, they camped in town?"

Hetty pointed to the lower end of the street, to the three vacant shacks Shawn had noticed as he rode in. "Last house — the Mason place. Living in there. Use the middle one for their horses."

Starbuck settled his gaze on the end structure. A lamp burned somewhere inside, and after a moment he saw movement behind the dirt-streaked window. He grunted, satisfied.

"Looks like they're set for the night," he said, and turned back into the lobby.

Hetty hesitated. "If you like, I'll stay here, keep watch."

"No need," he replied. "They'll be looking for me, but I expect they've had enough until morning."

Hetty Pierce laughed, and together they returned to the dining room. Simon had disappeared and Patience, on her hands and knees, with scrub brush and bucket of soapy water, was cleaning the mess on the floor. She straightened up as they entered.

"Everything all right?"

"Everything's fine," Shawn said, and with a thankful sigh, sat down and began to eat.

Hetty fell to helping her mother, first assisting with the cleaning chore, then removing the dishes and scraps from the table the outlaws had used. The food was excellent, done to perfection, and Shawn, after days on the trail eating his own cooking, made the most of each bite.

Halfway through, muted voices in the lobby snared his attention. Immediately he got to his feet and crossed to the connecting doorway, a quick caution laying itself upon him. . . . He could have figured wrong about the outlaws. Perhaps they weren't waiting until daylight after all.

It was Simon, along with several bearded men and a few elderly women. They ceased their talking when he appeared. Pierce, stepping forward, lifted his hand for attention.

"This is Mr. Starbuck," he said. And then turning to Shawn, "Like to have you meet these folks." He pointed to a lean, very erect man with a sharp, heavily lined face, alert black eyes, and snow white hair and beard.

"This is Oram Grey, our Senior Elder."

Grey extended a horny hand, gravely clasped Shawn's fingers in a surprisingly strong grasp. The man would be at least eighty — possibly more, Starbuck thought.

"Glad to meet you, Mr. Starbuck."

"My pleasure," Shawn replied, thinking of the wedge of apple pie cooling all too rapidly on his table. He shifted his attention to the next man, one of only a few years less age. He was small, had an apple-round head, craggy features, and long trailing moustache to match a spade beard.

"Jaboe McIntyre. He looks after our feed and seed warehouse. Runs our grist mill."

His grip, too, was strong. Starbuck looked to the next individual.

"Micah Jones, our blacksmith, and jack-of-all trades. Can make just about anything a man wants, and does — including the hide shoes we wear."

There was no difficulty in determining Jones's calling; large, thick torso, powerful shoulders and arms, he could have been nothing else.

"Ezrah Vinsent, the storekeeper where supplies are kept."

Hetty had spoken of Vinsent, Shawn recalled. Something about him being the only available bachelor in the valley. . . . Seventy years old, she'd said. He had an odd shade of blue eyes, sandy hair, and a ruddy complexion. Short and squat he could be no taller than Hetty herself.

"There're a few more Elders but they ain't around right now. Oram's son, Tolliver, and Charlie Crissman, to mention a couple."

Starbuck bobbed his head. "My pleasure to meet all of you. Now, if you'll excuse me, I'll —"

"We've been told of your encounter with the men who have moved in on us," Oram Grey said in a deep-toned, carefully modulated voice. It was evident he had received better than an average education — a tribute apparently to the quality of the Hebrenite schoolteachers. "I fear you have let yourself in for great trouble."

Shawn's shoulders stirred indifferently. "Something I've gotten used to. . . . Now, if you'll excuse me, I'll finish my supper. Was a pleasure to meet you all."

Wheeling, he returned to the table, sat down. Shortly the talking in the lobby resumed.

He finished his meal, superbly topped off by the apple pie and a second cup of coffee — which undoubtedly was something of a luxury in the valley because it was an article that had to be brought in — and rising, looked expectantly toward the kitchen. Neither Hetty nor

59

her mother were in evidence to accept his pay for the meal. Dropping a dollar on the table, he pivoted on a heel and made his way through the lobby to the street.

A coolness had settled over the land and the pale glow of a three-quarter moon was lighting the fields and softening the harsh, square lines of the buildings, and transforming the country beyond into a silvered, undulating sea. . . . Far up the valley a cow lowed mournfully.

The warm, velvet quiet of the night, the good smells of the earth, the muted noises — it all made him think of Muskingum, of the farm along the river, and of the times long ago.

His mother, Clare, tall, her gray eyes filled with those shadows that lent them a mysterious beauty, would be finishing up in the kitchen after the evening meal. His father — strong, iron-willed yet strangely sentimental — would be smoking his pipe in serene contentment as he sat in the chair he'd built under the apple tree that shaded the house.

And Ben — solemn faced, intent, and stubbornly independent — likely he'd be off to himself, dreaming the dreams that were to take him away soon after their mother died.

It would have been a quiet hour there, too. Cool and pleasant, with the kindness of night closing in silently to bring an end to day. Chickens would be murmuring sleepily on their roosts. The cows and big-hoofed thick-bodied work horses — animals with bottom, his father would say — could be heard munching solidly at their rations of grain in the barn. Overhead the last crows would be stringing raggedly across the dark sky for their night's perch in the tall sycamores growing along the river.

It had been a good life despite the hard labor and the occasional violent clashes of will between Ben and their father. . . . And then one day it was all over, it was of the past. He was grown, footloose, searching the length and breadth of the land for a brother who was never there.

Was there any use, any point in continuing such a seemingly hopeless quest? Should he heed those who often told him that he was wasting his life away, frittering the young years into old age, to awaken suddenly one day and find life gone and he with nothing to show for it? Should he —

Motion inside the old Mason house at the end of the street drew his interest. Lamplight lay against the window in a yellow sheen, filled the rectangle of the doorway and spilled out into the small front yard. Bobby Joe stepped into the open, stood quiet in the deepening night, face turned toward the hotel. Shawn, not certain if the outlaw could see him, held himself still.

Something was said by one of the outlaw's companions inside the structure. Bobby Joe wheeled lazily, sauntered back through the doorway, and was lost to sight. . . . Could the outlaws be planning to seek him out, square accounts that very night after all? He still doubted it. They would wait, pick a better time, hoping for a moment when they would not be expected.

As if to verify that conclusion, the light in the shack winked out. Shawn continued to watch the place for another five minutes, both the front and a portion of the building's rear being visible in the moonlight, and when he saw no movement, concluded he had nothing to fear until morning. Coming about, he entered the hotel.

There was still no one in sight as he crossed the lobby, mounted the stairway, and entered his quarters. Simon had been there. A large wooden tub stood in the center of the room. It was filled to half capacity. Alongside stood two buckets of additional water. Several thick towels and a bar of soap lay on the bed.

The Pierces — at least Patience and Hetty — had gone all out to show their appreciation for what he had done. When it came to Simon, he wasn't so sure. Nor could he be certain about Oram Grey and the other Hebrenite Elders. He saw no thanks in their eyes and heard no words of praise when he met them in the lobby.

It didn't matter. Tomorrow he'd be gone, and the Hebren Valley would be behind him — just a recollection. Shrugging, he pulled off his clothing, stepped into the tub. The water was cool, refreshing, and taking up the small brick of soap, he began to scrub himself. After a thorough going over, he reached for one of the buckets, poured its contents over his head, and settled back, enjoying the pure luxury of the moments.

An ease crept in, possessed him, relieving the tension, the stiffness of sweat and dust, the dull ache of muscle and bone put to test during the encounter with the outlaws. . . . It was good to just soak, let his mind lie idle, not think.

He remained in the tub for a good half hour, then rising, toweled off with the coarse cloths provided, and drew on a clean pair of light drawers. After that he dug out his razor from the depths of the saddlebags, and despite the lack of hot water, scraped the stubble of whiskers from his face.

He took the next few minutes to check over the contents of his pack, rearranging for convenience's sake as well as taking note of the things he needed and that, hopefully, he would be able to obtain from the settlement supply store in the morning.

Finally satisfied, he sat down on the edge of the bed, pleasantly tired, relaxed, and at peace, and thought about the Pierces and the rest of the persons living in Hebren Valley. That they faced a serious crisis was undeniable.

It boiled down to simple facts; they could not retain possession of the valley, continue the pacifist way of life they fancied unless they were willing to fight to preserve it — and this they could not and would not do. Violence was no part of their creed — even if the avoidance of such cost them home and all possessions.

And regardless of the outcome of the problem with the outlaws, the day was coming when the secret of the valley's location would be out. The word would leak somehow, and in a land spreading westward hungrily, with thousands of hopeful souls seeking land and a new life, it would be impossible to preserve the immunity.

The quiet rap of knuckles on the door brought Starbuck to his feet. He remained motionless for a time until the careful knocking sounded again. Quietly, he drew on his pants, and lifting the forty-five from its holster hanging from the bedpost, he crossed to the door.

Once again the rapping came, insistent but cautious. Shawn laid his hand on the knob. "Who is it?"

"Oram Grey," a low voice replied. "Important that I talk to you."

☆ 7 ☆

Shawn turned the key in the lock, drew back the door. Oram Grey, his lean face bleak and drawn, stepped inside quickly, closed the panel with his shoulders.

Starbuck, irritation showing in the tightening muscles of his jaw, eyed the man narrowly and dropped his pistol back into its leather sheath. He was tired, was looking forward to a much needed rest — and in no mood for a dressing down over the encounter he'd had with the outlaws. He hadn't asked for it; it had simply come to him and it wasn't in him to back off when pressed. If that went counter to the Hebrenite way of life, it was simply too bad.

The elderly man crossed to the washstand, reached up to the lamp bracketed above it, and turned up the wick, brightening the flame. He nodded to Shawn.

"Eyes are not what they used to be — and I like to see a man good when I'm talking to him. Can read the truth in his face sometimes when you can't hear it."

Starbuck's shoulders stirred. Crossing his arms, he leaned against the wall, features patient.

"Know it's late," Grey murmured, "and that you're tired. But this is important to me — to everyone in the valley. I hope you'll listen."

With no particular show of interest, Shawn said, "What's on your mind?"

Oram Grey reached deep inside himself for a full breath, squared his slight frame. "I need your help."

"Mine? Don't see how I can help."

"Way you handled those outlaws is proof that you can — if you will. Simon Pierce told me — all of us — what you did. Came to me that you were the answer to the problem that threatens my people."

A stir of suspicion moved through Shawn. "Meaning what?"

"You can rid us of them."

Surprise jolted Starbuck. He studied the older man closely. "Thought you were against a thing like that. Way Simon talked, you'd do anything to avoid violence."

"Simon told you what is true — and you'll get no thanks from the other Elders, or even the Family —"

"Then how is it you, the leader of them all, can ask me to fight — kill, actually, because that's what it'll take — for you?"

Oram Grey turned about slowly. Drawing aside the curtain, he stared into the paleness outside the window.

"Comes a time when a man must make a choice for the good of those who trust in him.

We are against violence, yes. Our history is that we have often moved, forsaken all we owned and held dear, to avoid it."

"Then how can you justify asking me to fight for you now?"

"Before the others, I can't. To myself I can. I feel honestly in my heart, that it is best. I am going against my own principles, and those that I teach and advocate, and that have been drilled into us all from the beginning — but for the good of all I believe it must be done."

Starbuck considered in silence. Then, "Nobody else knows about this — your coming here, I mean?"

The old man shook his head. "No one. And should you agree to my offer, no one must ever know what I did, that I hired you to do this job."

Shawn again leaned back against the wall. "I'm not a gunslinger."

Grey's black eyes were small points beneath their shelf of shaggy brows. "Even if it meant saving the lives of many fine people?"

"Hardly come to that —"

"Afraid it will before it's done with. This Kilrain who is coming will take his advantage of us and our beliefs. He knows we are pacifists, that we will knuckle under and not oppose him and his men. Thus they will be able to do with us as they wish."

"Answer to that is to send word to the nearest lawman, have him come in, take care of them for you."

Grey said, "No," quickly, as if alarmed. Then, "That would prove as fatal to us as the outlaws themselves. It would reveal the location of the valley, and we would soon be overrun by outsiders —"

"Most outsiders, as you call them, aren't like this Kilrain and his bunch. There're a lot of fine people around looking for a place to stop, build a home, who'd be a credit to your valley."

Oram was silent, reserving whatever thoughts he had on the matter to himself. Then, "Will you listen to my offer?"

Starbuck moved away from the wall, the weariness riding him, dragging at his tall frame. Nodding patiently, he sat down on the edge of the bed.

"Already told you how I feel about it, but go ahead."

"Thank you," Grey said. "As I've pointed out, we'll be helpless before a man like Kilrain and the ones who'll be with him. Not that we're afraid; fear has nothing to do with it. It's simply that we have no understanding of violence and it's against our nature and upbringing to involve ourselves in it.

"However, with all that is happening — our young folks leaving, our people growing old, dying out — I feel that I should take steps to preserve our way of life. . . . I owe it to all those who have gone before me, and to those who now look to me for guidance."

"Meaning you would sanction violence in

order to preserve a sect that is against violence?"

"In plain language, yes. That is where you could help. The need is to rid the valley of the outlaws — those who are here now as well as Kilrain and the others he is bringing with him. Once here, they must not be permitted to leave. If we let them escape, they will tell others of the valley and it will no longer be a haven for us."

"Which adds up to killing them all — every one of them."

"I'm afraid so. It's the only solution."

Shawn considered the old man, feeling a thread of compassion course through him. Oram Grey, the trusted leader, the infallible teacher and chief advocate of the peaceful life, recognized the inadequacy of this belief when threatened by the presence of a ruthless outlaw gang; and so dedicated to his people and their faith was he that he was willing to compromise himself and his ideals to preserve that faith.

"You must understand that the others in the valley can never know that I came to you — the reasons undoubtedly are clear. For your services, you will be paid well. I don't know how much money you would expect. The amount is entirely up to you — and it will be met. Cash will be available when my son and the others return from selling the cattle."

Starbuck shifted wearily. "I'll say it again, I'm no hired killer."

"Not like I was asking you to rid us of men,

but of scum-rats the country'd be better off without."

"Not questioning that, but a man's a human being regardless of whether he's good or bad."

"But if the price was high enough —"

"Got nothing to do with it!" Shawn exclaimed angrily, rising. "You don't have enough money to turn me into a murderer! Nobody has."

"Even when it means so much to many — to half a hundred honest, hard-working, God-fearing people — who without your help will be at the mercy of these outlaws?"

"Don't put it on my back. Go to the law."

"You can be the law. I'll appoint you as our town marshal. Nobody must know, of course —"

"Still be murder — and I'm not about to pin on a paper star and masquerade as a lawman to cover it up. Be willing to help in any other way you want. . . . Somebody said you thought Kilrain and the others were army deserters. When I ride out, I can swing by the nearest post, advise the authorities, and have them send a detail to pick them up. Or I'll find a sheriff or federal marshal for you."

"No — we'd be no better off. The valley would be overrun. It no longer would be ours — a secret place where we can live in peace."

"You're going to lose that secret anyway, no matter how it works out, same as you need to make some changes in your thinking. Backing away from trouble won't work in this world today. Everything's changed."

"I realize that, but after all that's been taught the Family, the — the code we've learned to live by. I just can't suddenly turn my back on the faith and tell them it's all wrong."

"You're only fooling them, making it harder when you don't. Faith's a fine thing, but it won't keep others from coming here, and it sure won't keep outlaws from running over you. Best thing you and your people can do is face up to the facts — in one way or another you've got to fight to live the way you want."

Oram Grey again looked through the window. Off in the distance a light moved slowly, jerkily across a field; someone with a lantern.

"There's no chance of you changing your mind?"

Shawn shook his head. "No — not to do what you're asking."

Grey moved slowly toward the door, a bent, very old man under the massive burden that had abruptly fallen upon his frail shoulders. He paused, one hand resting on the knob.

"Obliged to you for listening. Somehow I feel better."

"Only wish there was a way I could help. The army or some lawman — that's the only answer. They'd keep it quiet if you'd tell them."

"Perhaps, but there'd be nothing for sure.

And Kilrain and the others — they'd talk if only to spite us."

"Expect you're right there."

Grey turned to the door, drew it open a small crack, once more hesitated. "My coming here — talking — you won't mention it to anyone?"

"You've got my word," Starbuck said, and watched the man look right and left and then step out hurriedly into the hallway. "Good night."

There was no reply from the leader of the Hebrenites.

☆ 8 ☆

Starbuck closed the door, turned the key. He wished there was some way he could help Oram Grey and his followers — short of accepting an under-the-table job as a killer — but there appeared to be nothing he could do. His suggestion to Oram that he get in touch with the army or the law had fallen on deaf ears, and beyond that he could see no way in which he could be of service.

Hiring out as a gunslinger was not his idea of a job. During his search for Ben when it had been necessary to find work, he had done many things — stagecoach driver, shotgun guard, deputy sheriff, trail boss, plain everyday cowhand, wrangler, and many others, but never had he contracted to be an assassin — and he wasn't about to begin now.

Coming about, he reached for the lamp to turn down its wick. Weariness was dragging at him with leaden weights, dulling his thoughts, slowing his movements. It would be good to crawl into the bed, get a full night's sleep. He'd head out in the morning as soon as he could get supplies together and straighten out his directions.

He paused, rubbed at his jaw, wondered if anyone in the valley would know where the Carazones Peaks lay; it was possible no one would because the members of the Family, as they were called, were never permitted to leave. He shrugged. Someone, surely, would at least have an idea where —

He halted dead in the center of the room as again a knock sounded on the door. He frowned, wondered if Oram Grey had returned, had a different proposition in mind. . . . The answer would be the same; he was not going to let himself get involved.

The knocking came again. Wheeling angrily, he took up the forty-five once more, crossed to the door, and flipped back the lock. Pulling open the panel, he stepped back, surprise hitting him hard. It was Hetty Pierce.

"Shut the door — hurry!" she said in a quick, tense voice and brushed by him into the room.

Starbuck did not move, simply stared at her. She was clad only in a nightgown and some sort of light cotton wrapper, had it pulled about her body. Her hair — freed from the severe bun into which it had been gathered — now cascaded about her face and neck and down onto her shoulders in dark glistening folds.

She gave him an impatient glance, stepped past him, and taking the door in her hands, closed and locked it herself.

"I've got to talk to you," she said, facing him. "It's important."

It seemed to be a night for talking, Shawn thought, continuing to study her. He shook his head. "Hardly the time or the place — or the way to come dressed for that."

"Had to wait until ma and pa were asleep. . . . Anyway, I'm eighteen, or almost. I don't think you're much older than that."

"Maybe not in years but where I've been and what I've seen makes me about twice your age."

"No difference," Hetty said airily, sinking onto the edge of the bed. "I was listening out-side — a little. I heard you and Oram Grey. Why didn't he want you to say he'd been here?"

"Reasons of his own," Shawn answered, won-dering just how much the girl had actually overheard.

She made a gesture of dismissal with her hand. Then, "You're leaving in the morning?"

He felt a thread of relief. Hetty evidently had caught only Grey's last words. The old man's secret was safe.

"My plan. Could be Bobby Joe and his friends will have other ideas."

She took a deep breath, squared her small shoulders. "I'm going with you."

Starbuck did not permit his reaction to her words to show. He considered her quietly, im-passively. The yellow lamplight touched her cheeks, creamed them to a softness, and made her eyes much darker. She was a pretty girl, he thought again.

"Not that easy done," he said, moving toward the window. There had been a note of desperation in her tone and he feared to be blunt with her.

"Why not? I can ride — and I'll be no trouble. Just let me go with you until we come to some town, then I'll look after myself."

"Doing what?"

"I can cook, or maybe I can get myself a job as a waitress in a restaurant. I could clerk in a store. I've heard the freighters say there are big stores in the towns where they have a lot of clerks. . . . Why, there's a hundred different ways I could support myself!"

"You've never been in a town so you can't know what it's like. Take my word for it, it's not that easy."

"I don't expect it to be, but others manage it. I can, too."

"Life's plenty hard. Country's never yet recovered from the war — and that's ten years ago — eleven actually. Every job has a dozen people standing around waiting for it. I know — I have to hunt one up pretty often — and it's a lot easier for a man to find work than a woman."

"I'll make out," Hetty said stubbornly. "I've just got to get away from here! I'll go stark mad if I don't!"

"May seem that way to you. Best you remember that here you've got a roof over your head, people to look out for you — and you al-

76

ways know where your next meal is coming from."

"And that's all! There's nothing more! I heard you tell papa yourself that you couldn't live like that, all penned up. Do you know what's in store for me if I stay?"

Starbuck's shoulders stirred heavily.

"I'll end up wedding Ezrah Vinsent, that's what. He's the only unmarried man in the valley — and he's seventy years old. That's almost four times my age!"

"You won't have to marry him. They can't force you."

"Oh, yes, they can! It's a sort of rule. A girl must marry, produce children. It's the only way they can keep the Family going. And since there aren't any boys my age — they're all years younger — it leaves only Ezrah."

"You've been told it's to be that way?"

"Oram Grey's mentioned it to papa — that I'm of marrying age and that Ezrah needs a wife and me a husband. Next time he talks to him he'll ask that a date be set and want to know if the honeymoon rooms are ready for us."

Shawn frowned. "Honeymoon rooms?"

"That's about all the hotel's for. It's the custom for newly married couples to have a week here. They're given their choice of the rooms and move in right after the ceremony. Everything's brought up to them, and they don't leave — just stay put. Then when the week's over, they go to live in the house the Family has provided for them."

The Hebrenites had it figured down to a fine point Starbuck thought. Nothing was left to chance.

"What happens if you refuse to go through with the wedding?"

"Nobody ever has, but they'd have it their way eventually. The Elders've got the say-so over everybody. They're never opposed — not in anything they decide. And papa's one of them."

"You mean he'd go along with what Oram Grey and the others ordered whether you liked it or not?"

"He'd have to. He's got no choice either. Sometimes I think I'd be better off to just give in to Bobby Joe, let him have me."

"Bobby Joe — the outlaw?"

"That's who I mean. He keeps trying to catch me when I'm off by myself. A couple of nights ago he tried to force my bedroom window. I threw a bowl of soapy water in his face. . . . I'm afraid of him but it could be I'm wrong about him. One of the women has taken up with Abe, another of the outlaws —"

"Esther?" He was merely mentioning the name she had dropped.

Hefty looked at him in surprise. "Yes, Tolliver Grey's wife. How did you know?"

"Something you said earlier. Her husband is the one heading up the cattle drive."

"That's him, only don't make it sound like he was a young man. He's sixty or better, and Esther's only thirty-five. . . . Everyone around here is so old — the men, I mean."

"Don't Oram and the Elders know she is living with this Abe?"

"She doesn't live with him — she just sneaks out whenever she can, day or night — and meets him. I'm sure Oram doesn't know about them. I don't think anybody does except my folks and me. We've seen them meet and then watched her come home at all hours."

Shawn rubbed at his jaw. "Your pa being an Elder, it's a wonder he doesn't say something to her about it."

"I expect he has but he'd never mention it to us. . . . I — I'm sorry for Esther. I understand how she feels and I think I know why she has to do it. We're all in a trap here."

"Can't say she was very choosy about who she took up with."

"How could she be? They were the first outsiders many of us had ever seen. And they're young and strong. I'm grown woman enough to know that's what Esther needed. Tolliver may be younger than his father, but you'd never know it. He seems every bit as old."

"What happens when her husband returns?"

"Who knows? Esther'll probably go right on meeting Abe Norvel every chance she gets — could be she'll run off with him. And Tolliver won't do anything about anything. He won't

put up a fight for her, I mean. The men are for-
bidden to do anything like that. They're supposed to just sit back, talk things out in a
peaceful way."

"Beats a shoot-out, I expect."

Hetty looked at him closely. "Would you
agree to such an arrangement?"

Starbuck shifted his eyes to the window.
"Well, no, not my idea of —"

"You see! It's not my idea either! If I ever
have a husband, I want him to love me and
want me enough to fight for me — even kill for
me if he has to. I'm not going to be a piece of
livestock to be bargained over, parceled out. . . .
That's why I've got to leave here, Shawn, get
away, make a life of my own, and find the kind
of man that suits me.

"My folks — and the Elders — they don't realize that the Family is dying out, that there
soon won't be any of the sect left. They'll pass
on and all of the young people will have gone
away — and there won't be anybody left.

"And I can't stay here and become the wife
of an old man I hate! That would mean I'd be
trapped here for the rest of my life with nothing
to think about but dying. I'll do like Esther before I'll let that happen!"

Impulsively Hetty came off the bed, moved
up to where she faced Starbuck. She was very
close and he could hear the quick pound of her
breathing, smell the warm womanly sweetness
of her.

80

"I've got to go with you, Shawn. . . . I'll die if I can't! Will you let me? I'll pay any price you ask — any."

He was silent for a time, thinking of many things, thinking, too, of what the future held for Hetty Pierce in the valley, and was understanding her hopelessness.

"What about your folks?" he said then, breaking the hot stillness. "Wouldn't be right for you to run off without telling them."

"Papa will never agree," she said dispiritedly, looking away. "He has to stick by the rules. Mama will say I'm right — I'm sure of that. She can see what is happening and she'd want me to go because of the outlaws and what will happen when they take over."

Starbuck swore silently. The last thing he wanted was to be burdened with a girl when he pulled out in the morning — assuming he was able to do so. But he was finding it difficult to refuse her. It meant life itself to Hetty Pierce. She was like a caged bird frantically seeking to escape, and he could not deny that freedom. But he'd not do it under a cloud.

"It'll have to be all right with both of them," he said. "You get them to agree and we'll pull out together first thing in the morning — unless Bobby Joe and his bunch stop us."

Hetty's lips parted into a smile and her eyes brightened. "We won't have to worry about them! There's a path behind our barn. Runs west, clear to the foot of the mesa, then turns

81

south. We can get to the gate by taking it — and nobody will even realize we've gone."

"You know this trail? You've been over it?"

"Dozens of times! Everybody has except the outlaws, of course."

"It leads to the mouth of the canyon?"

She nodded. "I've been there, rode there by myself several times, intending to leave. I always got scared and changed my mind. I didn't know what I should do once I was outside the valley — no idea of where to go."

"It's the one we'll use — and I'm glad you mentioned it. Like to avoid making trouble around here if I can."

"Well, you can easy, unless they just happen to be looking and see us leave, or for some reason, miss us. If that happens, it could be a problem because the trail down the valley is a lot shorter. They could ride on ahead, cut us off."

"Up to us to be careful then, and starting early is a good guarantee."

"I'll be ready when you say —"

"*You'll* be ready if your folks agree to it. I'll want to hear it with my own ears. Also, I've got to gather up a few supplies — grub."

"I'll put what you need in a sack, have it all fixed for you. Save time. Expect you ought to have bread, meat, pickled fruit, things like that. Don't think there's any coffee left, not much anyway."

"Forget it. I've a few beans left. Main thing's

food — what you listed."

"I'll add whatever else I think you can use. There was something else you said you had to do —"

"Find out how to get to the Carazones Peaks country, and a ranch owned by a man named Hagerman."

Hetty shook her head. "There's nobody around here can tell you that. The freighters might, but they're both away on the cattle drive."

Starbuck only stirred.. He'd half expected that. It appeared he'd be forced to cut north to one of the forts or settlements after all, if he was to get his sights lined up right. It would be better now, anyway; he'd be able to get Hetty settled and off his hands that much quicker — assuming the Pierces allowed her to go.

"About five o'clock, that be when you'd like to start?" she asked.

"Be fine."

"Everything will be ready —"

He considered her narrowly. "It's understood now, isn't it? No point your being there waiting unless your folks tell me it's all right."

"I'll tend to that. Mama will agree, I know, and I'm sure she'll be able to persuade papa."

"But you said, him being an Elder —"

"Don't worry, mama can do most anything with him once she sets her mind to it," the girl replied, and reached for the top button of her wrapper. Her face was intent, her eyes shining bright. "I made you a bargain, Shawn, said I'd pay whatever price you asked. . . . I'm ready to pay now."

Starbuck stood wholly still. He had realized to some extent how important escape from the valley and freedom was to Hetty, but it had not occurred to him that it meant this much. Dark, hard-cornered face expressionless, he took her fingers into his hands, stopped their fumbling with the wooden buttons.

"You're one hell of a lot of woman, Hetty Pierce," he said gently, and leaning down, kissed her on the lips and stepped back. "There — now we're square. You've paid off in full. . . . Good night."

Stepping by her, he unlocked the door, held it open. She stood in the center of the room as if transfixed, staring at him in disbelief. Suddenly tears flooded into her eyes, and cheeks flaming, she hurried past him and disappeared into the hall.

☆ 9 ☆

Alone in her barren room, Hetty stood at the window, and staring into the pale lit night, sobbed for a reason she could not exactly explain to herself.

She had lied to Shawn, lied for the first time in her life, and that, she sought to assure herself, was the source of her tears. But she knew better. He had refused her — had treated her as a child — and that cut deep. And then like a shaft of light, the truth came to her. He had refused her not because she was less a woman but because he was more a man. Had Shawn been Bobby Joe or someone like him, the situation would have ended differently.

She felt something deep within her stir at that realization, and immediately her thoughts flew back to those moments when they had been together, and a warmness flowed through her. . . . She knew now — and Shawn must be made to understand, to recognize the feeling that had sprung up between them.

Turning from the window, she dashed the drying tears from her cheeks and crossed to the row of pegs on the wall from which her few pieces of clothing hung. Choosing the one dress she considered her best, she folded it carefully, laid it on the bed.

Then gathering up other bits of personal apparel, she put them and the dress into the handbag she'd knitted and lined with a remnant of flowered percale someone had given her, and hung it on the bedpost.

Going to the doorway, she entered the hall, quietly made her way past her parents' bedroom to the porch on the back of the hotel. Opening the closet where her father kept his spare work clothing, she selected a butternut shirt, a pair of pants — faded and shrunk from many washings to a size that would come nearest to fitting her — and a ragged-brimmed, hand-woven hat of straw. Folding all into a bundle, she returned to her quarters.

There she donned the rough garments, finishing off the garb by pulling on a pair of the thick-soled work shoes made by Micah Jones and provided by the Family for members to use when they did their periodic stints as field hands.

Taking up the knitted bag, she went back into the hall and headed for the kitchen. She spent a good quarter hour selecting and assembling the food items that Shawn wanted for the trail, placing them in a muslin sack used for grain, and left it on the table. After that she let herself out the side door and made her way to the barn.

Resolute, she entered the stable and singled

out one of the four horses standing in their stalls. She backed the animal, a thick-bodied, heavy hoofed black used by the teamsters, into the runway where the light was better, and saddled and bridled him.

Affixing the knitted bag with her belongings to the patched hull, she led the horse to the doorway. She started to mount up, was taken by a second thought. Leaving the black, she returned to the hotel, slipped quietly down the short hall to her parents' room. It wouldn't be long until time for them to be up and about, she knew, and she was taking a bit of a risk, but it had to be done.

Entering, she crossed in the darkness to her mother's side of the bed. Placing a hand on the older woman's shoulder, she shook her gently. Patience opened her eyes at once. Hetty held a finger against her lips for silence.

"Just want to tell you I'm riding up to the lake to pick berries. Going early before it gets hot. Tell Mr. Starbuck I put the things he wanted in a sack. It's on the kitchen table."

"Things?" Patience echoed drowsily.

"Food. He asked for it. . . . Tell him good-bye for me."

Simon stirred restlessly, partly awoke. Patience nodded, settled back.

"I'll tell him," she murmured thickly.

Hetty drew off, studied her mother's slack care-lined face for a long breath, resisting the urge to place a farewell kiss upon the older woman's cheek for fear of rousing her again and possibly creating a quick suspicion. Wheeling, she returned to the hall and to the waiting black.

Satisfied with the charade that she felt would allay all questions relative to her absence when the morning came, she climbed onto the saddle and swung the horse toward the trail that led into the west. The hull was much too large for her and the stirrups too long, but she'd not worry about that now. She'd adjust them later. At the moment her mind was soaring with the thoughts of what lay ahead for her — beyond the valley.

A town — a street with rows of stores running down each side, filled with things she'd never dreamed of, peopled with smiling, friendly folk who waited to welcome her. There'd be clean, neat little homes scattered about on green hillsides, brightened with flowers, shaded by huge trees, all lived in by happy, laughing couples who loved each other and who married because of that love and not as a bounden duty arranged by dried-up, bearded old men who cared only that children be the result of their union.

It would be heaven living in such a world, Hetty was sure. She'd never actually seen what it was like outside Hebren Valley, but she had looked at the pictures in the magazines the freighters brought in — or did until Oram Grey put a stop to it because he said it gave the young members wrong ideas and made them dissatisfied.

Oh, it would be truly wonderful to be free, to live in such a glorious world!

☆ 10 ☆

Starbuck was awake and dressed well before first light. Moving to the window, he glanced at the sky. . . . Another scorcher of a day coming up. Motion in the street caught his eye. A woman on a small pony was just moving into the shadows near the feed warehouse. Esther Grey, he guessed idly and turned back into the room. Collecting his belongings, he tucked them into his saddlebags, entered the hall, and quietly made his way below to the kitchen. He found the sack of provisions Hetty had prepared for him, and leaving several silver dollars on the table to settle his bill, hurried to the stable. Saddling and mounting the gelding, he located the path the girl had spoken of, moved off, secretly pleased that he had disturbed no one and that Hetty had not been there, waiting for him.

The sorrel, frisky after the night's rest and feeding, pranced show-horse style along in the cool, half light. It was with difficulty that Shawn restrained him from breaking into a lope and setting up a hollow beat on the baked ground that would be heard in the settlement.

The land was no different here from elsewhere in the West, he noted. The moment he pulled up out of the valley with its cool springs and streams and gained the flat sandy heights above, his surroundings changed.

The grass lost its lushness, turned from rich green to grayish thin clumps. Large trees became nonexistent, replaced by cedars and other scrub growth designed by nature to survive the heat with a minimum of moisture.

The fertile, dark soil was loose now, studded with rock; and the metamorphosis of the country itself was from one of tranquil, prosaic farming to a friendless, rugged world of wild, fierce grandeur. He was only a short distance from the floor of Hebren Valley, yet it was as if he had removed himself a thousand miles.

Such was no novelty to Shawn. In his search for Ben, he had whipped back and forth across the impatiently stirring West, from the Mississippi to California's Russian River, from the sleepy *pueblos* south of the Mexican border to the frozen plains of Montana. He'd come to accept change and difference as part of life, just as he had learned all men vary not only in appearance but in thought and ideals and in their estimation of values.

He thought of Oram Grey at that moment, of his lonely despair, his need to do what he felt was necessary for his followers even at the cost of his ideals. To the leader of the Hebrenites any means to an end evidently was justifiable as long as it compromised only him.

Starbuck looked ahead. The trail, having followed an almost due west course, was beginning to veer south, meander along the shale-cluttered base of a line of red-faced bluffs. The valley, deep green and shadowy, was below and to the left.

The villagers would be up by that hour, preparing for a day's labor in the fields or whatever communal duties had been assigned them. Shawn stared thoughtfully at the faint band of pearl showing along the eastern horizon. Was that the way men were intended to live, as Oram Grey and his Hebrenites believed?

Was living as a single family, each person having no more and no less than another — with all delegated and sharing labors that contributed to the welfare of the whole rather than to the individual — was that the way it was supposed to be? Was that the true and satisfying life?

It hardly seemed so to him. A man was nothing in that sort of arrangement, no more than a cog in a machine, a solitary straw in a broom. What was there to an existence such as that?

Gently, he eased back on the gelding's leathers, mind suddenly cleared of all thought, finely tuned senses keenly alert. A short distance along the trail, behind a shoulder of rock, his eyes had caught a hint of motion. An animal of some kind, perhaps — or it could be a man.

Reaching down, he moved the holster on his left thigh more to center, let his hand rest on the weapon's smooth walnut butt. The pearl in the east had changed now to a rose-orange flare, and around him the land was losing its softness and the harshness of reality was reclaiming the starved brush and heat-blasted rock.

Slowly he drew abreast the slab of sandstone. Above it was only the steep barren slope. If it was a trap, there would be only one rider involved; the shoulder was not large enough to conceal two. . . . He grinned faintly; the thought of Bobby Joe and his friends waiting somewhere along the trail was making him unduly edgy. Likely it was a deer — or possibly a cougar. The big cats liked those rock ledges.

But Starbuck was not a man to accept probabilities. Guiding the sorrel in close to the formation, he drew his pistol and halted.

"You — back of that rock! Move out where I can see you."

At once he heard the dry creak of leather, the slow thud of hooves. The head of a pony appeared, and then its rider. Shawn swore softly in surprise. It was the woman he'd seen crossing the street earlier that morning — the one he assumed was Esther Grey.

He considered her coldly, slid the forty-five back into its holster. "Good way to get shot. What were you doing there?"

She raised her head, looked directly at him. She was an attractive woman with a wealth of hair that was the color of panned gold, full curving lips, and large, light eyes that, being somewhat slanted, gave her a faintly Oriental appearance.

"Waiting for you."

Starbuck sighed quietly. "Expect that means you're wanting to leave the valley, too."

Her brows lifted. "Too? Is there someone else going with you?"

"Wanted to."

"Who?"

"Don't see as it matters. You're Esther Grey, I reckon."

She nodded. "I'd like to ride with you to the next town, if you don't mind."

Starbuck shrugged. It appeared he was slated to have company whether he wanted it or not. First Hetty and now Esther — and he couldn't very well refuse her.

"Expect you know there's a chance I might not leave the valley. Your friends could be aiming to head me off."

"I don't think they know you're gone," she said.

"What I was hoping. Surprised to see you. Thought you were all set to go with them — leastwise, with the one called Abe."

Esther looked off into the valley. "I — I decided to go on now — with you."

Shawn gave her words passing consideration. She and Norvel had evidently quarreled, causing her to change her ideas and plans.

"Is it all right — my riding with you? I have

my own food and water, and I'll not be in the way. I have to go. I just can't stay in the valley any longer."

He could understand that to remain there as the wife of Tolliver Grey and the woman of Abe Norvel would create an impossible situation for her, but he had his doubts about her future just as he'd had for Hetty's.

"You realize what it'll be like on the outside?"

"I haven't been out of the valley since my parents brought me here — a long time ago. We came by wagon train from Nebraska, but we never stopped at any of the towns, always avoided them, so there's very little I know of things."

"You'll not find them the way you think they are."

Esther Grey stirred dispiritedly. "I don't expect to. They never are."

"What can you do — what sort of work, I mean?"

Like Hetty Pierce she probably planned to work as a waitress or a cook — the jobs there were always more than enough applicants for.

"I can teach school," Esther said. "That's what I was trained to do in the valley."

"Fine," Starbuck said, relieved. "Chances are you'll make out. And you're old enough to know what you want — and what you're doing."

"I do — for years. It's just been a matter of

waiting for someone to help me — to take me, really — out of that prison."

"What about your husband and children?"

"He's part of the prison — and there are no children. There's no reason why I should stay. I don't fit. I never have and it's doubtful I'll be missed — even by the man who is my husband if he were there. . . . Are you letting me ride with you? I'd go on by myself only I wouldn't know which way to turn once I was free."

"If that's what you want," Starbuck said, and glanced to the east. A small edge of the sun was breaking over the ragged skyline.

"Best we get started. Going to be a long, hot day."

He touched the gelding with his rowels, sent him trotting on down the trail. Esther swung in behind him, and shortly they were moving steadily along the gentle grade.

They rode in silence, Esther wrapped in her own thoughts, Shawn looking ahead, weighing the probability of trouble at the mouth of the canyon guarding entry to the valley. If the outlaws had discovered that he had pulled out and were determined to stop him, they would make their play at that point.

There was no assurance it mattered enough to them one way or another whether he rode out or not. They would always carry a grudge for him, of course, but it wasn't likely they'd go to any great lengths to settle it. And as for his departure from the valley, they would probably view it as good riddance. Maybe luck was still with him.

Again he reined in the sorrel, a quick, sharp oath springing from his lips as they rounded a bend. Waiting in the center of the trail was Hetty Pierce.

☆ 11 ☆

Clad in a man's clothing several times too large for her slight frame, Hetty greeted him furiously.

"So this is why you wouldn't let me come! You were bringing her — and you didn't want me tagging along!"

Starbuck, temper on a short fuse at being saddled with one woman and facing the prospects of a second, swore angrily, said, "The hell! Found her waiting on the trail, same as you."

Hetty glared at Esther suspiciously. "A likely story — and I'm noticing that you didn't make her turn back."

"She's a grown woman, old enough to know what she's up to."

"And I'm not —"

"No, by God, you're not!" he replied bluntly.

Hetty recoiled slightly from the sharp impact of his words. She folded her arms across her breasts, settled herself stubbornly on the out-sized saddle girthed to the plow horse she was riding.

"Well, you're taking me, anyway. If Esther can go, I can, too."

Shawn sighed helplessly. "Expect the best

thing we can all do is turn around and go back, forget this day ever started. If we ride fast enough, maybe we can get there before either one of you is missed."

"Only one who'll miss her," Hetty said acidly, glancing at Esther, "is her outlaw lover."

The tall woman smiled patiently. "I'm afraid that's all over — ended."

"Good! You ought to be ashamed —"

Again Esther smiled. "Why should I be ashamed of something that was good and natural? To Abe I was something besides another pair of hands to work in the fields, someone who wasn't a teacher or a cook or a drudge to take care of a house — I was a woman."

Hetty's eyes spread indignantly. "You've got the nerve to talk about it, to flaunt —"

"No, I'm just trying to explain, but it's something you'd never understand."

"No, I never will! You had a husband and you were carrying on with that outlaw —"

"I was married to Tolliver Grey. He was never a husband, at least not what I think a husband should be. And after we learned I couldn't bear children for him, it became worse — less a marriage. I might as well have been dead."

"You were still married, no matter what," Hetty insisted firmly. "You ought to've remembered that."

Esther stirred listlessly. "I couldn't expect a child to understand —"

"I'm no child!"

"Of course you aren't," the older woman said coolly. "What price did you offer to pay Mr. Starbuck if he'd take you with him?"

Hetty wheeled to Shawn. "You told her!" she cried cheeks flushing wildly.

"He told me exactly nothing about you — not even that you wanted to leave," Esther said. "But I know my kind — and I know what hopelessness can do to a woman caught in its trap."

Her voice broke. She turned her head, looked off to the south. Freedom lay in that direction and her resolve to find it was mirrored in the brightness of her almond-shaped eyes, the firm set of her lips.

Shawn rode out the silence that had fallen between them for a full minute, then nodded. "If you two've got all the poison out of your craws, we'll do a little sensible talking. . . . Still think you'd both be smart to turn back."

"No," Esther said at once. "I'll ride on alone, take my chances, before I'll go back to the valley."

"So will I," Hetty declared.

"All right," Starbuck said resignedly. "We'll go on. Keep remembering this, though. We're still not out of here. Hard to say what could be waiting at the mouth of the canyon."

"He means your outlaw friends," Hetty said, glaring at Esther. "They're all worked up because he had a fight with them — beat them —"

"No only them," Shawn said. "Could be your

pa and a few of the Family Elders — if they've found out you're missing."

"They won't," Hetty said promptly. "Told my ma I was going berry picking. They won't expect me back for hours."

Starbuck looked away, suppressed a smile. Hetty had done a lot of figuring. Turning back to her, he said, "Don't pay to be too sure of something like that. Could be they weren't fooled."

Hetty wagged her head stubbornly. "They won't be there. . . . I know."

Shawn was silent for a moment, then glanced up to find Esther studying him. The sun was out in full strength now and its light caught at her hair, turned it to the color of the marigolds that grew so profusely on the slopes.

"When you were around Abe and his friends, they mention anything about me, like keeping an eye on me, things like that?"

The tall woman said, "No, nothing. But I didn't see the others last night — only Abe."

"I see. . . . You happen to know their last names?"

Esther's eyes showed some surprise. "Why, yes. Bobby Joe's is Grant. And it's Rollie Lister and Abe — or really Abraham — Norvel. Why? Is there some reason —"

"Nothing special. Just wondered if I'd ever heard of them. Seems not."

He wondered at the relief that flashed across her features, and then riding forward a few strides, raised himself in the stirrups and looked off toward the end of the valley. The small, narrow canyon that lay at its beginning would be just beyond the ridge he could see looming up hazily in the distance. It would be wise to avoid the valley entirely by swinging wide and coming in to the canyon from below the ridge, he decided. They would then be only a short distance from the exit.

Wheeling about, he explained the situation to the two women, and finished with, "Important we go quiet so let's have no more of this wrangling between you two. We keep to the brush and stay off the high spots on the trail. Once we're in the canyon, we'll have to be twice as careful. Understood?"

Esther nodded. Hetty said, "We'll be careful," and then, "Shawn, everything will be fine once we're out of the valley, won't it? I mean, there'll be no more trouble — no need to worry —"

"Nothing much," Starbuck replied, heading back onto the trail. "Just Indians — Comanches and Kiowas both — a sun that'll fire up to over a hundred, short water rations, and no idea of where the nearest town is. Outside those few minor items, we'll have no problems. . . . You both ready? Let's go."

Under his breath he sighed heavily. How the hell could he have gotten himself jockeyed into a situation like this? Two runaway women — one fleeing from a husband who meant nothing to her, the other escaping her parents and a marriage to a man she feared and despised — both desperate to abandon a life they could no longer bear. And to top that off there was the possibility of having to fight his way — and theirs — through the guns of three outlaws.

All he'd wanted was information and a small stock of provisions so that he could continue on his way. How did it end up? As usual, with someone else's troubles on his shoulders — two quarreling women at that!

He reckoned he could stand it. Such occurred in one form or another, it seemed, from time to time, and he always managed to survive although there'd been a few occasions when there'd been doubt. . . . But two contentious, perverse women. . . . He grinned wryly at the realization. If they weren't at each other clawing and scratching like a couple of bobcats disputing territorial rights, he'd be plenty surprised.

Twisting about on his saddle, he gave the pair a long look, noting Esther's set, resigned features, Hetty's stubbornly defiant expression.

"If you two are smart," he said, "you'll cut out that feuding and get together. Thing to do is find a good town, get yourselves jobs, and share a house. Won't be so hard or so lonesome if you'll do it that way."

"I'll never get lonesome for the valley!" Hetty declared immediately.

Shawn plucked at his ear. "You'll be surprised how soon you'll start thinking about all the good things and wishing maybe you could live them over again. Happens to everybody when the nights get long and it's quiet and you can't sleep. . . . Can even happen in the day — the remembering how it was."

"I'll never feel that way — never! Will you, Esther?"

The tall woman brushed at her eyes. "I don't know. Right now I don't think so. I think only of the bitterness I found there."

"Well, you can bet I won't be sorry. I hate the valley. I'll be so glad to be far away from it that I'll welcome anything — everything!"

Starbuck made no further comment. He slid a careful glance to the sun, now well on its way to the midday mark in the empty sky. Heat was rising steadily. They would be forced to halt soon, let the horses rest.

There was little shade of consequence to be seen on the slope they were crossing, but at the foot of the ridge that separated canyon from valley, he could see a dark band of growth. There could be a spring. If so, it would be a good place to call a halt.

They reached the tiny oasis late in the morning. The spring was small, furnished water only for the horses, which Starbuck led up, one at a time.

He drank sparingly from the half-filled canteen he carried. It was still some distance to the larger creek below the canyon where he planned to refill both containers, but he was unworried. There was water in the area and that was a satisfying knowledge. Too, Esther had provided herself with a gallon jug that was full and which she offered to share with Hetty. The girl accepted it without hesitation, seemingly forgetting her acrimonious feelings for the yellow-haired woman for the moment.

They took advantage of the shade to rest and eat a little of the supplies Shawn had brought, and an hour later were again in the saddle, following a faint path that climbed steeply to the top of the ridge.

Once there, the trail as steeply dropped off onto the yonder side, and in short time they were down in the narrow canyon with Hebren Valley, at last, behind them and lost to view.

That realization seemed to visit each of the women, and both were abruptly silent as if for the first time they were facing up to the fact that they were leaving the past behind, had crossed, finally, a river of no return.

It was their problem, Shawn thought, singling out the mouth of the canyon with its improvised gate now visible in the distance. He would suggest once more that they change their minds, return to their sheltered havens in Hebren Valley — and let it drop. If they decided to go back, all well and good; if they chose to continue with him, he'd do what he could for them and make the best of it. He wouldn't lose any large amount of time, anyway; he was forced to cut back to one of the settlements for directions, regardless. He'd leave Hetty and Esther there.

The trail angled sharply to the right, began to follow the edge of a deep arroyo that sloped down from the higher plateaus to empty into the stream flowing along the floor of the canyon.

The gate was definite now. The brush lashed to the framework, long since dried, was a flat sage-green, and from where they were, it stood out in stark contrast against the still growing shrubbery. Looking back, he pointed to it.

"That's the way out. You're free once you're on the other side of it. Either one of you wants to back out, now's the time to do it. Be your last chance."

Esther Grey, features expressionless, shook her head. Hetty, toes pushed into the stirrup loops instead of the too low wooden bows, lifted herself, looked to the north.

"Not me. . . . I'll never be sorry. . . . Never."

Shawn resumed his position. "Sure hope not," he said. "Leaving home's a big jump. I know because —"

Stiffening with alarm, he hauled up on the sorrel's reins as three riders burst from the dense brush dead ahead.

"It's Bobby Joe — the outlaws!" Hetty Pierce screamed.

"Down into the arroyo — jump!" Starbuck yelled, drawing his pistol.

Gunshots rattled through the hot stillness. He felt the gelding shudder, stumble, was suddenly leaving the saddle in a soaring arc as the big horse went down. A white hot force slammed into the side of his head — and then blackness engulfed him in a vast, soft cloak.

☆ 12 ☆

The brutal, penetrating lances of the noon-day sun brought consciousness back to Shawn Starbuck.

Face down in the arroyo bed, he opened his eyes slowly, caution stilling any outward movement of his body until certain he was alone.

He could hear nothing but the drone of insects, the far-off mourning of a dove. Sweat bathed him completely, and there was a stinging along the left side of his head, an uncomfortable stiffness to the skin. His left shoulder ached with a persistent throb. It must have borne the full brunt of his fall.

Where were the others — Esther and Hetty, the outlaws?

A shaft of panic hit him, sent a stream of fear coursing through him. Hetty — in the hands of Bobby Joe and his partners. . . . And Esther — she'd be no better off if she was no longer of interest to Abe. Moving only his eyes, he stretched his vision to encompass as much of the immediate area as possible. He saw only the glistening sand, the thin weedy growth, and a gray mottled lizard panting rapidly beneath a rock at the edge of the arroyo.

He sucked in a long breath, winced at the pain the effort evoked. . . . He couldn't just lie there, wait for darkness. That was hours away. He'd not survive the heat, and the two women — he groaned, thinking of them. He'd have to gamble — hope luck was with him.

Twisting his head slightly, he turned his face an inch at a time to the opposite side, straining to catch any sounds that would indicate the nearby presence of the outlaws.

He was alone in the arroyo. A few feet away the head and neck of the sorrel hung over the lip of the wash, the remainder of the gelding's body still on the flat above. The big horse had been dead when he hit the ground, Shawn guessed.

Slowly he sat up, making no sound. The outlaws could be in the lower end of the arroyo. Flat on his rump, legs extended in front of him, Starbuck paused. A wave of nausea swept over him. He held himself rigid until it passed and was replaced with a steady stabbing pain in his head.

He raised a hand, gingerly touched the burning, aggravated area above his ear with fingertips. . . . Dried blood and a tenderness such as he'd never known. . . . He lowered his arm, sat there thinking. He remembered then. A bullet had slammed into him, striking a glancing blow just as the sorrel had started down. He'd been pitched off the saddle, thrown hard into the arroyo ten feet below.

Starbuck muttered an oath. It was a wonder he was alive. The bullet from the outlaw's gun had missed being a killer by the merest fraction of an inch. And the fall — there was no good reason why it hadn't provided him with a few broken bones.

He continued to sit there, motionless, still somewhat stunned, with the sun beating down upon him while he waited for a second spasm of giddiness to pass and a degree of strength to return to his enervated body. Then, easing forward, he got to hands and knees and slowly crawled to where the head of the sorrel hung into the arroyo. The gelding's lips were pulled back, revealing his broad yellow teeth. It was as if he were snarling defiance at the sudden death that overtook him.

Pausing for a long minute, still listening, striving to pick up any signs of life close by, Shawn drew himself upright. Again the nausea claimed him while a host of needle points dug into his brain.

He ignored it all as best he could, hanging on patiently, doggedly, knuckles of his hands showing white as he clung to the rocks in the arroyo's wall, until the sickness once more passed. Slowly then, he drew himself up as far as he could. He was unable to see over the edge of the wash.

Worn from the attempt, he glanced around seeking a break in the wall or a lower area. He could see none and moved back then to where

110

he was directly below the dead sorrel. A fairly large rock jutted from the gravelly soil offering a foothold, while a clump of groundsel — yellow flowers blooming raggedly — suggested purchase for his hands. . . . If he could manage to reach that far up, he should be able to grab a part of the sorrel's saddle — a stirrup, perhaps — pull himself to where he could look onto the flat.

There was no saddle on the gelding.

Balancing on one foot, clinging grimly to the slowly yielding clump of brush, sweat streaming down his face, he stared at the horse. The outlaws had removed his gear. He looked down at his middle hastily, swore vividly. Belt holster, gun — all were gone. He guessed he would have noticed it sooner except he was still a bit thick from the rap he'd taken from that grazing bullet.

But he was alone. He got that much satisfaction out of the effort expended in climbing up halfway. The flat to the east of the wash with its stand of brush, out of which Bobby Joe, Abe, and Rollie Lister had come, was deserted in the hot sunlight.

Again ignoring the shocking stabs of pain, he threw himself forward on his belly, clawed to catch the sorrel's mane. He felt the coarse strands between his fingers, locked tight upon them. Then, digging toes into the arroyo bank, he drew himself over the lip of the deep cut onto the level of the flat.

Panting from exertion and pain, drenched with sweat, he sprawled alongside the sorrel. Flies were buzzing around the ragged wound in the animal's chest where the lead slug had ripped its way, and he unconsciously brushed at them with a hand, sent them pulling back in a dark swarming cloud. Whoever had fired the bullet that killed the gelding had got in a lucky shot, the lead slug had missed bone, gone straight to the heart.

Shawn felt a stir of regret and pity, and then relief for the sorrel. The red had carried him over a lot of country, had been a fine, dependable mount. He hadn't suffered, and if death was to come, that was the best way — fast and unexpected.

Breathing normally at last, he got to his knees, to his feet, and looked around, moving his head slowly to prevent a resurgence of the nausea. Evidently the outlaws had figured him for dead. They had noted all the blood on the side of his face, and as he was totally unconscious from that as well as the fall, they'd simply assumed they'd killed him, had appropriated his gear, taken the women captive, and moved on.

He felt the stir of fear within him again as he thought of Esther and Hetty being in their hands. Esther, of course, was older, wiser, could probably take care of herself pretty well. . . . But Hetty Pierce — and with Bobby Joe hungering for her the way he had — He rubbed

112

at his jaw, tried to think.

Where would they go?

Back to the valley — that seemed logical. But again, there could have been a change in plan, and with the two women at stake, he couldn't afford to be wrong. No one knew exactly what the outlaws had in mind, he had just drawn conclusions from scraps of information picked up here and there. For all he knew they could have left the valley or have decided upon another place nearer the entrance to hole up. . . . He had to be sure.

Starting forward, eyes on the ground, he began to search for tracks. Giddiness overcame him and he caught himself, turned, and stumbled toward the darker green shrubbery that marked the location of the stream. He'd get some water, wash his face good. Be smart to let his head soak for a little. Should help it to clear. After he'd done that he ought to be in better condition to think.

It was a long, murderous hundred yards to the creek. He reached it on unsteady legs, sank down, and belly flat, lowered his face into its cool depths.

Water touched the raw wound in his head, stung sharply. He flinched, drew back, and again sank his face into the stream, this time with more care. An ease began to slip through him after a few moments. He sat up, removed his shirt, splashed himself, scrubbing away the sweaty coating of dust.

It would be fine to strip completely, crawl into the creek, and stay there for an hour or two. He'd feel better after that sort of a treatment for sure — but it was out of the question. He had to start moving, find the outlaws, get to them before they could harm Hetty and Esther. . . . And on foot, wounded, and with no weapon except the slim-bladed knife he always carried inside his left boot, he had one hell of a job ahead of him.

The brief respite had done much to improve the way he felt, and his head, bound now with a bandage made of his bandanna, had cleared. An unsteadiness still bothered his legs, caused his knees to tremble spasmodically now and then, but that he was sure would eventually pass.

Rising, he moved out into the brilliant sunlight to where the sorrel lay. There he scouted about until he located the prints where the horses had all come together into a small bunch. From there it was simple to follow them as they struck out, one in the lead, the remainder in groups of two. He visualized it; it would be Rollie Lister at the head. Behind him would come Abe riding alongside Esther Grey. They would be followed by Bobby Joe Grant siding Hetty.

They were returning to the valley. That could only mean they had missed him at the settlement after all his precautions, had hurried down the shorter trail that cut along the floor of the valley, and cut him off. He might have

made it if he'd hurried — if he hadn't been delayed. But there was no sense hashing that over
now.

What would they do with the women? Because they were apparently returning to the settlement, would they release them once they
arrived? Esther, perhaps, as she had come and
gone pretty much as she pleased. Hetty was a
different matter. She'd fought Bobby Joe from
the start, and she'd still fight him, and by so
doing she would make it impossible for him to
let her go.

He'd keep her there in the shack, and the
people in the settlement would never know of it
until it was too late. Then, when he and the
others had taken their fill of her, she would be
offered her freedom — or the opportunity of a
life as a woman for the outlaws.

Shawn shook off the thought, glanced to the
steel-arched bowl of the sky. The sun was directly overhead and bearing down its hardest.
They had at least an hour's start on him, possibly more. He looked ahead, up the canyon,
and moving hurriedly, crossed to the trail that
ran parallel to the stream.

The distance to the town by this route was
considerably less, he recalled, and it shouldn't
be too tough going. He broke into a slow jog.
He'd have water nearly all the way — shade
from the trees that grew along the banks of the
creek. . . . If only the sun wasn't so damned
hot —

In that next instant Shawn felt his knees buckle. A grayness came drifting into his eyes. Strength drained from his legs and he had the sensation of floating, tipping forward. Frantically he threw out his arms to save himself, failed, pitched full-length onto the hot sand.

☆ 13 ☆

Gasping for breath, plastered with sweat, Starbuck lay for long minutes. Finally, he rolled over, picked himself up cautiously. He'd overestimated his strength; he guessed he was worse off from that glancing bullet's blow and the fall than he'd thought.

Moving slowly, mystified by the strange sensation of lightness that gripped and refused to release him, he started for the creek. He couldn't recall having ever experienced the sense of irrelation that possessed him. On the few previous occasions when he'd been shot, it hadn't affected him in this manner.

The fall — he supposed that was it. Being thrown over the dying sorrel's head and landing hard on the solid floor of the arroyo ten feet below. It had been one hell of a moment for him. He was realizing that now.

But he couldn't let it matter. He must get his feet squarely under him and make it back to the settlement, locate the outlaws, and free the two girls. . . . And there was a little matter now of personal property to be recovered — the belt buckle that had been Hiram Starbuck's. He could replace the rest of his gear, but the buckle was something else, and he'd not quit until he recovered it.

He reached the creek bank, dropped to his knees. Brushing off his hat, he scooped a double handful of water, bathed his burning face. Removing the bandage, he dipped it in the stream's cooling depth, wrung it almost dry, and reapplied it.

He felt much better after that, and settling back, rested in the shade of the overhanging trees. But conscience would not permit him to enjoy the recess for long. Within short minutes he got to his feet, and cocking his hat to one side in order to avoid pressure on the stinging, throbbing wound in his head, he once again started up the canyon.

He had learned a lesson. No longer did he try to hurry, to pursue a plan of alternately walking and running, conceived earlier. Now he moved at a steady but not too hurried pace, keeping near the stream with its attendant growth. Occasionally he would halt, find a spot to rest briefly. At such interludes he would again bathe his face, soak and replace the bandage.

The day lengthened with the heat decreasing but little as he pressed on doggedly, climbing out of the canyon, topping the ridge, and finally dropping into the Hebren Valley. He lost the comfort of the adjacent stream there as the road cut away, followed a higher level.

But he did manage to stay within reasonable

reach of water and the healing qualities it seemed to offer. Several times he swung away from the twin ruts and crossed to where the creek flowed. It was time lost — but well invested; better to get there late than never at all. And the heat, even when he was near the water, lashed him mercilessly, sucking him dry and robbing him stealthily of strength.

But he would not give in despite the fact that the two women had worked themselves into their present predicament and perhaps should be left to get themselves out as best they could.

After all, the outlaws were their worry — theirs and Oram Grey's and all the other Hebrenites in the valley. Let them face up to what must be done, or if they persisted in living by the pacifist code they professed and wanted to just lie quiet — like a rabbit being chewed up by a coyote — then let them.

Too many times he'd permitted himself to become involved in the troubles of others. He was about due to back off, keep his nose pointed straight ahead, and go about his own business — that of finding Ben and getting matters settled so he could obtain his share of old Hiram's thirty-thousand-dollar bounty.

Then he could start having a life of his own. He could get himself a good piece of land, start a ranch — the Circle S he'd call it. He'd go in for cattle and good horses, specialize maybe in that big tan-and-cream-colored breed he'd seen down in Mexico — *palominos,* they were called.

Beautiful, proud animals they were. They made a man's pulse quicken.

Shawn's rambling thoughts died. He pulled to a stop on the crest of a low hill, surprise rippling through him. The edge of the settlement was visible, the squat bleak shacks that stood at the end of the street were just ahead.

He pulled back hastily, hunched behind a clump of sedge. He could see most of the street — the fronts of the buildings. No one was in sight; the place had the same frightened, deserted appearance as before.

He settled his attention on the three shacks. The old Mason house, as Hetty had termed it, was the first in line. The outlaws were using it as their quarters, she'd said. The second, or middle structure, had been converted into a stable for their horses, while the third was empty.

No life was evident around any of the shacks — not even a horse — and that realization sent a spurt of alarm through him. Had the outlaws turned off somewhere between the canyon and the town? Could they have gone on after all, having made a change in plans and left the valley?

He shook his head. He still didn't think such was likely. The idea, according to what Simon Pierce and the others had overheard, was for them to wait for Kilrain and the rest of the outlaw bunch; they'd not pull out until the others arrived.

The men could be inside, the horses around in back or possibly inside their improvised stable. From his position on the hill, he was too far to the front to see the rear of the structures. Taut, worry nagging at him, he dropped back below the crest of the hill, circled wide, and keeping to a small gully, trotted to a point where he figured he'd be provided with a view of the opposite ends of the shacks, and there climbed to the level of the land.

A sigh slipped from his cracked lips. The horses, all five of them, were tied to a sagging hitchrack at the back of the Mason place. The outlaws had returned to the settlement as he had assumed — and that they had not released either Hetty or Esther was evidenced by the presence of their horses with the others.

He mopped at the sweat on his face, glanced to the sky. Not long until sunset. It had taken hours — the entire afternoon — to walk from the canyon to the settlement. He reckoned he was fortunate to make it at all, however.

Now, whatever he was to do must be done at once. Cutting back to the gully's depth, he followed it out for a short distance to where it flattened to meld with the mesa and again sought out a small knoll that would afford him a view of the houses.

He wasn't too far from them, he discovered with satisfaction — a hundred paces, perhaps a bit more. Scouring the intervening ground with probing eyes, Shawn located a second arroyo, somewhat larger, to his right that angled toward the structures. By keeping down and moving close to the west bank of the wash, he could manage to get in close.

At once he drew back, crawled down onto the still hot floor of the arroyo. Ignoring the throbbing in his head that the bent position summoned, he covered the distance to where he was near the first house as rapidly as possible.

Breathless, head swimming, he drew back against the low embankment, allowed the giddiness and throbbing to fade. . . . He should wait for darkness, he thought again, before climbing out to the level of the yard behind the shacks, but the clamoring urgency within him would hear of no such delay. He'd simply have to risk it in daylight.

Mopping away sweat and breathing back to normal, Starbuck pulled off his hat, raised himself slowly, and peered over the rim of the arroyo. He was midway between the vacant house at the end and the one being used as a stable. The Mason place where the men were holed up was at the far end.

That was good. Gathering his legs under him, taking up his headgear, he came out of the arroyo in a quick leap, and hunched low, dashed across the open ground to the near corner of the empty shack.

Keeping close to the back wall of the vacant house, he crossed behind it, spurted across the narrow yard to the converted stable, and then made his way to its lower side. There he paused to listen, to reassure himself that his presence was still unknown. Convinced, he moved quickly across the last bit of open ground to the rear of the Mason place.

The neglected horses, slack-hipped and dozing at the rack, did not stir as he drew in behind a clump of rabbit brush and squatted on his heels. Sweat was glistening on his face, trickling down his back and chest, and the throb in his head was a steady pounding.

Raising a hand he brushed at his eyes, cleared them of the salty moisture gathered in their pockets, and tried to see through the smudged, dusty window of the house. He could hear the low mutter of voices but it was not possible to locate exactly where inside the shack the speakers had gathered.

He settled back. He'd come this far, taken his chances — and the breaks had been with him. Maybe luck would continue to hold in his favor. Sucking in a deep breath, he sprang from behind the dump and raced to the corner of the old Mason place.

Taut, he listened. There had been no change in the voices, plainer now but still unintelligible. The men, he guessed, were in a room at the front of the house. Still low, he moved forward, halted at the window in the back wall. Again removing his hat, he rose slowly, brought his eyes to a level with the dust-covered sill, and looked through the dirty glass.

Relief flowed through him. It was a small room. In one corner a ragged mattress had been piled. Sitting on it, gagged, hands and ankles bound, was Hetty Pierce.

☆ 14 ☆

Where was Esther Grey?

Cautious, still unable to pinpoint the position of the outlaws, Starbuck drew back. Head below the window's ledge, he moved on across the rear of the weathered old house toward the door that was standing open.

Reaching there, he again dropped to hands and knees, and hat off, peered around the corner. The entrance was into the kitchen. The voices were coming from a room beyond it. Squinting, he could distinguish Abe Norvel and Bobby Joe in what was apparently the parlor. Rollie was there also, heard, but hidden from view by an intervening wall.

He saw Esther then. The men were grouped around a table playing cards. She was sitting behind Norvel. She spoke as Starbuck watched, but her words were inaudible. When she had finished, Norvel glanced to Bobby Joe. The younger man shook his head after which Esther lapsed into silence.

"If you ain't turning her loose, then what are you doing with her?" Norvel's words reached Shawn clearly.

Bobby Joe spread his cards on the table,

leaned back. "Aiming to keep her right here," he said, and then jabbed a thumb at Esther. "That there yellow-haired gal of yours'll have company."

"You mean you figure to keep her penned up in that back room like a sheep?" Rollie Lister asked.

"Sure, 'til she gets wised up and wants to stick around of her own notion — like Abe's gal. Only take a couple of nights, then she'll be willing."

Rollie's tone was doubtful. "We best be thinking about the rest of the folks around here. They find out we got her — and Abe's gal — they're just liable to rear up and do something about it."

"Like what?"

"Like using a pitchfork on one of us. Man standing in the dark and throwing one of them things can be mighty wicked!"

"Not them. Ain't enough spunk amongst the lot of them to put out the fire was their britches burning."

"Ain't so sure," Abe said doubtfully, and turned to look at Esther.

She got to her feet, walked slowly into the kitchen, and sat down on a sagging bench placed against the wall.

Rollie Lister said, "Can tell you one thing for goddamn sure, Kilrain ain't going to like it — not one bit! You know how he feels about having women around."

"He'll be changing his mind once he sees what we got corraled."

"What *you* got," Norvel said quietly. "You can pass that kid around if you like, but Esther's my woman. Making that plain here and now."

Bobby Joe laughed. "Now, I ain't so sure she's all that much yours! She was taking off with that there Starbuck fellow, wasn't she, right along with the kid. You sure she won't go running out on you again?"

Abe made no reply. Bobby Joe slid a glance over his shoulder at Esther, whistled admiringly. "Got to admit she's a real humdinger — but don't you go letting yourself get all roped and tied. Ain't going to be no time for courting and marrying. Whoring around, yes, but nothing more'n that. You recollect back there in the guardhouse at Bliss when we worked all this out with Kilrain, we agreed we'd be like them guerrillas in the war — Quantrell's outfit — remember?"

Abe shifted on his chair. "Sure — sure."

"Said we'd hit and run and hide, taking what we wanted — which included women, and then dumping them when we was through with them. Expect you'll remember that, too."

"Sure, but —"

"Ain't no buts to it. That's the way it'll be and that's how Con will expect it to be. So, if you've gone and got yourself set on that yellow hair, you'd best get it out of your mind right

127

now. . . . Smartest thing you can do for yourself is have her all spread out for Kilrain himself when he gets here."

A chair scraped on the floor. Lister's voice said, "He ought to be showing up," and then the outlaw walked into view, crossing behind Norvel, pointing for the front door. "Six, seven hours late now."

"They'll be here," Bobby Joe said. "Prob'ly was late starting — or they could've run into a mite of trouble."

"Trouble?" Lister repeated, pausing.

"Trouble," Bobby Joe stated. "You forgetting the army's still hunting us? They could've bumped smack into a search detail somewheres. For all we know, Con's dead as old Starbuck or else back in the guardhouse, and all the others with him."

"You're a cheerful son of a bitch," Rollie said laconically, and continued on for the doorway.

Shawn, crouched outside the rear entrance, digested the information he'd overheard. Bobby Joe was correct in just about all of his figuring, Shawn conceded, except where he was concerned. He wasn't dead and he didn't subscribe to the Hebrenite creed — and there was something he'd do about it.

It meant sticking his neck out plenty. The odds were all wrong and he'd be laying his life on the line for people who, in fact, excepting Hetty and Esther, would not thank him for delivering them from their oppressors. Indeed they blamed him now for the violence that had occurred in their midst. They would condemn him for any more in which he became involved even though it was for their benefit.

He guessed he was a fool to consider doing it; in fact, for all the blessings he'd receive from the Hebrenites, he definitely was. But Shawn wasn't thinking so much about them as he was about Hetty Pierce and maybe Esther.

They were the ones who needed him; the women, plus the fact the law of the land was to be flaunted by this Con Kilrain who had dreams of being another Quantrell at the head of a pack of ruthless renegades. . . . Every man had a duty when he became apprised of such, and Shawn Starbuck had never felt he was an exception to that unwritten rule. . . . And then there was the matter of his own gear — of old Hiram's prized belt buckle.

Pulling back, he made his way to the window of the room where Hetty was being held captive. Rising again, he tapped lightly on the streaked pane. Hetty turned quickly. Her eyes spread with surprise and then filled with tears of relief. Shawn nodded reassuringly, but with no plan in mind, he simply motioned for her to remain quiet and not worry.

Moving back to the door, he once more took up a position there. Esther still sat on the bench, idly fingering the folds of her dress. Lister was at the front entrance. Bobby Joe and Abe Norvel still slouched around the table.

Afraid to trust Esther, Shawn stayed well out of sight as he tried to establish the arrangement of the shack in his mind.

The entrance where he crouched led into the kitchen. In that room's opposite wall an archway opened into a short hall off which lay the bedroom where Hetty waited, and the parlor. A fourth room, probably another bedroom, evidently was connected to that area. The front door, only a portion of which was visible to Starbuck, was placed near the center of the parlor's forward wall and opened onto a small landing and yard that faced the street.

Getting into the back room and freeing Hetty while the outlaws were in the parlor was out of the question. He would have to come up with something else besides trying to slip by them — and Esther. She was an unknown quantity and he couldn't risk depending upon her for help.

There was also the problem of a weapon. He must locate and recover his belt and pistol; the rest of his gear could be picked up later — assuming everything worked out and he was still in need of equipment. But a pistol or his rifle was absolutely essential; he could accomplish nothing against the sort of odds he was going up against without a gun in his hand.

He needed to draw the three men, and Esther, out of the house; that was the answer — and the big chore. Once that was done, he could slip in, recover his forty-five and release Hetty, and get her out of the house. Esther, too, if that was what she wanted.

He wondered about the tall, yellow-haired woman. Would she leave if she had the opportunity? She had been running away from the valley, and Abe Norvel, when he encountered her on the trail. Would she again accept the chance to flee? He wished he knew the answer to that. He'd know then if he could trust her. As it now stood, he was afraid to include her in any plans he might make.

"Somebody's a coming!"

Lister's voice broke through to him. He pivoted his attention to the doorway where the outlaw stood.

"Somebody?" Bobby Joe echoed. "Your eyes getting so bad they can't tell who it is?"

"Maybe," Rollie answered, and pushing open the dust-clogged screen, stepped out onto the landing. For a long minute he stared off into the lower valley, shading his eyes from the glare of the setting sun with a hand cupped over his brow.

"Con and Shep —"

Bobby Joe and Norvel got to their feet, started forward. The younger man said, "Just them? Ought to be more."

"Well, there ain't," Rollie drawled, and moved on out into the yard with Bobby Joe and Abe trailing after him.

☆ 15 ☆

Starbuck came to attention. If all three men would move into the street, or even well out into the yard, he'd have the opportunity he sought — not a good one but at least a chance to enter, free Hetty, and grab up a gun.

Esther. . . .

His jaw tightened at thought of her. She was still there in the kitchen, blocked his way. He'd have to risk it — and if she made a move to warn the others, he'd have to stop her. He glanced again to the yard through the open doorway. The men were sauntering into the street. At that moment Esther rose, walked to the archway, stood there back to him, watching. At once Starbuck came to his feet. Entering swiftly, he closed in behind the woman. Throwing one arm about her waist, he drew her tight against him, clamped a hand over her lips.

"It's Starbuck," he said in a whisper. "I'm here to get Hetty. You want to stay — or come?"

He felt her tense body slacken with relief. She managed a nod. He released her. "Out the back — wait."

As Esther turned away, he cast a glance to the street. The outlaws had halted, were all facing to the south. Driven by the need to accomplish hurriedly what he had set out to do and be gone, he stepped into the short hallway, cut sharp to the door at its end. Opening it, he moved in and bending down drew the knife from his boot and slashed the cords that bound Hetty's wrists and ankles.

Pulling down her gag, he said, "The back — hurry."

She stared at him, eyes worried. "You're hurt! We — Esther and I thought you were dead —"

"Talk about it later," he snapped. "Esther's waiting in the back for you."

Immediately he wheeled into the hallway, again threw a look to the street. Bobby Joe, Lister, and Abe Norvel had not changed position, still watched the road that led up the valley.

Shawn glanced about hurriedly. He had only moments, he knew — but he must have his gun. His gear was not in the parlor or the hall. He moved deeper into the room where he could see into the adjoining area. His jaw clicked shut. Piled in the back corner were his saddle and other belongings.

Again shifting his gaze to the outlaws, reassuring himself they had not altered position, he crossed into the front bedroom. His belt and holster were not on the saddle. He swore angrily, then saw his pistol lying next to a holster and belt left by one of the men. Somebody had taken a fancy to the silver buckle, made an exchange.

He didn't quibble. It was a swap he'd rectify later at a more opportune time. Snatching up the strange belt, he wrapped it about his waist, jammed his weapon into the holster, and returned to the parlor.

Pulling up close to the wall of the room, he put his attention on the street. He could hear the slow regular thud of oncoming horses. Bobby Joe was grinning broadly. Abe and Rollie Lister's faces were wooden, devoid of expression.

Shawn spun about. He could see Hetty and Esther standing just outside the kitchen door. Moving silently and fast, he hurried to them.

"Want you both away from here," he said in a hard voice. "Rest of the bunch are here and it's —"

"What the hell took you so long?" Bobby Joe's bantering tones cut in on Starbuck's words. "You been dragging a dead cow all the way or something?"

"Or something," a voice replied. "What's the rush? You got something special good waiting?"

"Depends on what you're a thinking about."

"Well, after a year in that goddamn guardhouse it sure ain't no Sunday school picnic I'm looking for."

"Are they the rest of the outlaw gang?" Hetty

asked in a low voice. "Thought there'd be more."

"Seems they're all that's left. One's Con Kilrain, the other one's Shep, from what I heard. . . . You've got to hurry."

Moving by the two women, he pointed to the hitchrack. "Take your horses, lead them. Keep behind the houses. Long as they're standing in the street, you won't be seen."

Esther nodded, stepped to where her pony waited. Hetty paused, considered Shawn with a frown.

"Aren't you coming?"

"Later," he answered. "They've got some property of mine I aim to get back. Owe me a horse, too. Big thing is for you and Esther to get away from here."

Hetty did not stir. "You're not planning to fight all of them — you, by yourself?"

He grinned. "Not if I can help it, lady."

He shifted his attention to Esther Grey. She had freed the reins of her horse, was looking uncertainly toward the houses near the church. Hetty, stepping up to her mount and finally ready to leave, turned to her.

"What's the matter?"

The yellow-haired woman shook her head. "I — I don't know what to do. I can't go back to the house — to Oram — Mr. Grey — my father-in-law."

Starbuck peered through the doorway and the tunnel-like hall. The newcomers had pulled

135

up before their waiting friends, were now dis-mounting in the stiff, rigid way of men having been in the saddle for too many hours.

The older, dark-faced one with the grim, set mouth would be Con Kilrain, Shawn supposed. Shep was young, like Bobby Joe, had the same loose-jointed, uncaring manner to him. All would be entering the house shortly — and one of the group would lead the horses around to join those at the rack. Anxious, he swung to the women.

"Get moving!" He motioned impatiently to Esther. "Figure out somewhere else what you want to do. Go with Hetty to her place. You've got to get clear of here or I've done a lot of sweating for nothing!"

Hetty bit at her lip. "Not my place — I'm afraid to go home. . . . My folks —"

Shawn swore, took another look at the front of the house. The outlaws, walking leisurely, were coming across the yard toward the door of the shack.

"Go there anyway," he insisted in a low voice. "Tell them I'll be along in a few minutes and explain. That'll maybe keep them off your backs until we can come up with a better idea."

Hetty nodded reluctantly. Esther, giving the reins of her pony a jerk, started across the open ground.

"Go 'til you get to the other side of the next house, then cut alongside to the street. When you don't see them standing out front any longer, it'll be safe to cross over."

Hetty, trailing Esther, paused again. "Can't understand why you won't come, too."

"Told you. They've got my gear. I want it back."

Hetty looked at him narrowly. "You're not planning to slip off — leave me?"

Starbuck brushed at the beads of sweat gathering on his forehead. "Give you my word," he said tensely. "Hurry!"

Esther had reached the far side of the converted house, was leading her horse into the yard that separated it from the end structure. Shawn waited until he saw Hetty also round the corner and then stepped back to the doorway. Keeping low and being careful, he turned his attention to the interior of the shack.

Relief was easing the tightness that had gripped him; he'd gotten the two women safely away — and he had his gun. At least he could face Kilrain and his bunch on a halfway even basis. He had a quick wish that he could catch them all together in one of the rooms; he could manage them that way — the lot of them. Only luck wasn't favoring him that well.

Norvel was carrying something into the front bedroom — probably Kilrain's and Shep's gear. The outlaw chief and Lister were standing in the center of the parlor talking. Shawn's eyes whipped hurriedly about, he saw that Bobby Joe and Shep, evidently close friends, were still in the street engaged in laughing conversation.

137

His glance touched the sudden glint of silver at Bobby Joe's middle. Anger stirred him. It had been the young outlaw who'd taken his belt with the silver buckle. He'd not be wearing it for long. He brought his attention back to the men in the parlor, straining to pick up their words.

He needed some idea of what their plans were before he formulated a scheme of his own. . . . If they were aiming to ride out of the valley immediately to stage their first bullion wagon holdup, it would be simple to lay a trap for them at the gate when they returned.

But if they intended to wait, to hang around the settlement, complete their take-over, and prepare it for an outlaw stronghold, then he must set his thinking to other lines and act accordingly. That would call for catching Bobby Joe alone, recovering —

"Sure hate to hear that about Medford and Joe." Rollie Lister had turned, was facing the kitchen. His words were clear. "You getting somebody to take their places?"

"Naw," Kilrain said, sinking into one of the chairs. "They's five of us. That's a plenty — and the split'll be better." The man had a deep, drawling voice that showed a hint of Southern upbringing.

Shawn became aware in that next instant that Shep and Bobby Joe were no longer standing in the street. In that same fragment of time he heard the scuff of boot heels, the thud of hooves at the side of the house, and rose quickly.

Abruptly he was face to face with the two outlaws. Both men stiffened with surprise. Bobby Joe yelled, and both reached for their pistols.

Starbuck's hand flashed down, whipped up as he wheeled. His weapon blasted the stillness of the dying day, drove both outlaws back for the shelter of the building's corner. Pivoting fast, he legged it for the nearby arroyo.

☆ 16 ☆

Starbuck went into the arroyo in a low, flat dive. He struck the sandy floor hard, winced as the impact sent pain surging through his body. Breathless, he gathered his legs under him, hearing a wild cursing back at the shack as Bobby Joe and Shep made their explanations to the others.

"Only gun in town — that one." It was Rollie Lister's voice.

"He the one you said was dead?" Kilrain's question was dry, sardonic.

"Sure thought he was."

"Seems he ain't. . . . Get after him!"

Starbuck was already up, racing along the wash wishing it curved toward the settlement rather than to the opposite direction. His chances would be far better among the buildings, however few, than in the open.

"Yonder he goes!"

At Bobby Joe's shout, bullets splatted into the sand around Shawn's feet, thunked into the low wall of the wash. He threw himself to one side, dodging, ducking, looked about desperately for cover.

The back of the general store was fifty strides

140

to his left. Reaching it meant forsaking the comparative protection of the arroyo and exposing himself as he crossed the open ground that lay between — but it was still a better bet.

Ducked low, he raised his pistol, snapped two hasty shots at the shadowy figures moving toward him in the half dark, and lunged out of the wash. Whipping back and forth erratically, he ran with utmost speed for the shelter of the low-roofed building.

Guns crackled spitefully, steadily. Lead plucked at him, droned angrily by his head. He reached the structure, dropped in behind a large wood box attached to its wall.

Sweat was streaming off him. He was heaving for breath and his legs seemed to have lost all their strength — but he knew there was danger in remaining stationary. The outlaws would split up, come at him from two sides, have him cornered.

Still crouched to avoid silhouetting, he moved on, continuing along the wall of the store until he came to the street. If Kilrain and the others hadn't as yet divided forces, he should cross over. It would be easier to hide, get himself set if he could gain the opposite row of buildings.

He could hear the hard pound of boots coming from the direction of the arroyo. It was difficult to judge whether the men were still in a group or not. . . . It didn't really matter, he decided; he was forced to gamble, anyway.

Taking a deep breath he went to a low hunch, and spurting into the street, headed for the feed storage barn directly in front of him.

He reached it just as the outlaws rounded the back of the general store. Five guns blasted simultaneously. Bullets slammed into the weathered boards of the warehouse, clipped through the leaves of nearby brush.

Not hesitating, he raced on, came to the rear of the structure, ducked around its corner, and halted, lungs again crying for wind. He looked ahead. A short distance away was the blacksmith shop. Coals glowed dully in the forge and a thin trickle of smoke, barely visible, twisted up from the rock chimney into the thickening sky. But as it was elsewhere along the street, no one was in sight. The Hebrenite village was like a prairie dog town; at the first indication of peril, all evidence of life simply disappeared.

Beyond the smithy stood the taller bulk of the hotel with its stable aside and somewhat to the rear. From there on he was again faced with open country. Starbuck shook his head, finding no answer as to what his next move should be.

Bobby Joe shouted something into the night. An answer came from farther down the street. The men had separated, were beginning a sweep through the village in a systematic, army-forage-line manner, stalking him as they would an enemy.

He considered the hotel. It offered the most effective concealment but he hesitated to make use of it. Hetty and the Pierces would be inside, along with Esther Grey and possibly others. To enter could bring Kilrain and his bunch down upon them, expose them to injury and death.

Best seek a different place where, protected on at least two sides, he could have it out with Kilrain and his followers without jeopardizing the lives of the Hebrenites. Casting about, his eyes fell upon a sod shanty hunching half below ground level to the west of the blacksmith shop. It was apparently a storm cellar or storage room of some sort.

From it he would have a good sweeping view of the settlement and of anyone approaching from that direction as well as from the sides. To get at him from the rear a man would have to circle far wide and still would come within his range of vision.

Delaying no longer, Shawn broke clear of the wall along which he crouched, sprinted across the field, and jumped down into the slight pit behind the shanty.

"Here! Over here!"

Squatted low back of the hut, he heard the sudden yell, could not spot the man who had sung out because of the darkness. It sounded like Rollie Lister but he wasn't certain.

Moments later boots hammered in the street, then fell silent. The outlaws were gathering somewhere in front of the feed warehouse, or possibly it was the blacksmith shop. He couldn't tell for sure but there was no doubt they had him located.

He glanced to the western horizon. Complete darkness would soon envelop the valley and that would be of help. If he could hold out until then, he would be able to drop back to the brush a hundred paces to his rear, and under the combined cover of night and the scrubby growth, find a more advantageous point.

Just where that might be he wasn't sure, there weren't many places in the settlement where a man could fort up unless he went into one of the buildings, and that he was reluctant to do. He was an unwelcome and despised stranger among the Hebrenites now; he'd not draw them into the conflict and make matters any worse.

A shadowy figure appeared at the north corner of the blacksmith shop. Starbuck watched the man closely. Motion at the opposing end of the same structure drew his attention to that point. And then farther up, at the rear of the feed storage barn, the outline of a third man took shape.

They had spread out, were planning to move in from several points — five to be exact. He rubbed at his jaw; he'd spotted four of the outlaws — where was the fifth?

Worry began to tag at his mind. Had he allowed one of them to get in behind him?

Keeping his head down, he scoured the irregular alleyway along the buildings with care.

Only four half-hidden figures, growing more difficult to see with each passing minute, were visible. He could make out no sound or motion on the open ground behind him either.

Lamplight flared in the window of a house near the church, a single yellow square in a broad sea of darkness. The distant sound of a cow lowing came from up the valley, and inside the feed warehouse he could hear the muffled sobbing of a child. It hadn't occurred to him, but the men who operated the community's supply depots probably had living quarters in the rear of the buildings.

Abruptly he saw the fifth man — a slim, dark shape on the roof of the hotel. He had time only to jerk back, flatten himself against the short wall of the hut. The outlaw fired. Starbuck spat as dust sprayed into his eyes and mouth and nose. A voice yelled from back of the smithy.

"You get him?"

Another bullet thudded into the shanty's slanted roof. Shawn, stretched full length, hugging the mud brick wall, steadied his weapon upon its edge, aimed carefully, and pressed off a shot. The outlaw rose suddenly to full height, a stark figure against the sky, took a stumbling step forward and pitched over the edge to the ground.

Instantly Starbuck changed positions, knowing the flash of his gun pinpointed his location. Bullets smacked into the sod of the hut

145

and then Bobby Joe's voice lifted above the echoes.

"The bastard got Rollie!"

A dim figure emerged from the smoke and shadows to his left, unexpectedly close. Shawn threw himself back, full length, fired. There was a muffled curse and the figure ducked away, faded into the night.

A second shape began to materialize. Shawn drove it back with a quick shot, missed, pressed off another. It was difficult to see, to be accurate in the acrid-smelling gloom. With Rollie it had been different, he made of himself an easy target, but there in the black void behind the buildings it was another story. Motion caught his eye directly ahead. He tightened the trigger. The hammer of the forty-five clicked on a spent cartridge.

Hunched low, he rodded the empties from the weapon's cylinder, hastily thumbed fresh shells from the loops of the belt he wore, and started to feed them into the pistol's chambers.

Shock and dismay hit him. The shells wouldn't fit. They were of a different caliber. His pistol was a forty-five. The loops of the belt he'd grabbed up in the shack were filled with cartridges for a forty-four.

☆ 17 ☆

Angrily he threw the handful of cartridges aside. He hadn't given the possibility of their being a different caliber a thought — likely because there'd been no time back in the old Mason place to consider it.

He grinned wryly; Bobby Joe would be up against the same problem only he would be in a position to do something about it, either borrow a suitable weapon or get the proper shells from one of his partners. Chances were he had already discovered the difference and had done just that.

The vague figure in front of him that had drawn his attention had paused, was scarcely visible as the man crouched low. A faint clicking sound told Starbuck that he, too, had been forced to reload.

Shawn drew himself to hands and knees. One thing was certain; he must get away from the sod shanty and do so fast. With no means to defend himself, he would be at their mercy — and they would close in quickly, doubly determined to get him after he'd knocked Rollie Lister off the roof.

Rollie. . . . That was the answer. . . . Find the

147

pistol he had been using. If it proved to be of the wrong caliber, then get to Lister's body, take possession of his supply of shells.

Shawn holstered the useless gun, and bent low, crossed to the brush west of the shanty. There, partly concealed by the scattered clumps of rabbit brush and white-flowered plume, he angled for the rear of the hotel. Halfway a rustling in the heat-withered branches of the scrubby growth brought him up short. Abruptly a man was before him, arm upraised. Weak moonlight glinted on the weapon in his hand.

Starbuck hurled himself to one side as the pistol blossomed orange in the night. He felt the scorch of the bullet upon his arm, caught a fleeting glimpse of the outlaw's drawn face — Shep. He veered, drove himself straight into the taut shape.

They came together in a jarring collision. A yell exploded from Shep's blared mouth as Shawn's shoulder speared into his chest, bowled him over backward. An answering shout went up from somewhere near the feed warehouse.

Before Shep could yell again, Starbuck was upon him, pounding at his face, his head, and neck while his eyes searched frantically for the outlaw's weapon somewhere on the ground close-by. Suddenly Shep broke clear, rolled away.

"Over here!" he shouted.

A gun blasted through the night. The bullet struck something well beyond them, caromed off into the black with a high, shrilling noise. Shep cursed wildly.

"Don't shoot — dammit!"

Boots were thudding on the hard-baked soil. Shawn, still looking for Shep's pistol, continued to press the outlaw, driving him back, keeping him off balance with a steady hail of blows. He slowed, aware of the nearness of the others. They were close — too close.

Wheeling, he ducked low to avoid being seen, ran a short distance on a direct line due west to confuse Shep. Again reaching the edge of the cleared area, he darted into the scrub, swung once more toward the hotel. Rollie's pistol was still his one hope — unless it had been damaged in the fall.

Breath was rasping so loudly between his teeth he was sure he would be heard. Sweat blinded him and the ache in his head was a continuing pound of thunder. He threw a hurried glance over his shoulder toward the bulking structures along the street.

He could see no movement in the shadow-blotted flat behind them, but Con Kilrain and the others were there — somewhere — but just where it was impossible to tell. Bobby Joe, Norvel, the outlaw leader, and now Shep were roaming loose in the dark, could at that very moment be closing in on him unseen.

Stumbling onto Shep had been sheer accident, a measure of good luck. If it hadn't occurred the outlaw would surely have gotten in behind him — and chances were he'd not be among the living by then.

The high shape of the hotel was immediately to his left. He paused, glanced to the roof. Rollie's body should be lying near the corner. Continuing, he trotted to that pool of darkness spreading below the structure. Somewhere close-by unseen horses shifted restlessly. He halted, a stab of caution going through him — and then he remembered that Hetty and Esther had led their mounts to the rear of the hotel. Undoubtedly they were the source of the noise.

He moved on more slowly, stumbling through piles of debris. His foot came into contact with a solidness that gave against his toe — Lister. The man had fallen partly across the bottom step of the stairs leading to the landing.

Shawn bent swiftly, rolled the outlaw to his back. Moonlight, now gaining in strength, spread across the man's slack features. It was unnecessary, Starbuck knew, but he felt for Rollie's pulse, assured himself no life remained. It was a subconscious action; if Lister still lived, he would be entitled to aid, regardless.

But the outlaw was dead. Shawn began to probe about in the loose dirt and trash. A glint of metal a few steps away brought him about. He moved to the spot quickly. It was the pistol.

Grabbing it, he checked a cartridge. Another forty-four. His own belt of ammunition was still useless, but there was Rollie's. Returning to the body, he flipped back the tongue of the heavy brass buckle that locked the leather strap around the outlaw's waist, jerked it free. Almost all of the loops were filled he noted as he drew it into place.

Starbuck took a long, satisfying breath. He wasn't naked in a thorn patch any longer; he was again armed, ready to match Kilrain and his bunch bullet for bullet. Grim, he dropped back to the brush, getting as far from the hotel as possible so as not to draw the outlaw's fire in that direction if they spotted him.

He was not forgetting the child he'd heard crying inside the feed storage barn. It would have been one of Jaboe McIntyre's offspring. He hoped it and none of the other members of the man's family had been struck by one of the bullets that had sprayed the structure.

He halted in the pale light now spreading over the land, not certain what his best move would be. He could double back to the sod shanty, resume the stand he'd made there. It wasn't likely the outlaws would expect to find him at that location again.

Or he could swing completely around the hotel, cross the street at its lower end where darkness and distance and the smattering of brush would conceal his movements, and return to the Mason place. The horses were there. He could take his choice, collect his gear and ride out — leave Hebren Valley and its troubles quickly behind.

It wasn't his fight, anyway — at least, it hadn't been at the start. The outlaws had already moved in and taken over the town when he arrived. He'd be smart to get out of it, be on his way, let the Hebrenites cope with their problems as best they knew how — and in the manner they wished. They had experienced such crises in the past and come through them; there was no reason to believe they could not do so again.

But there was a big difference in the crisis confronting the people of Hebren Valley now and the uncertainties that had plagued them in earlier times. They were doomed to remain and endure persecution, not find relief and sanctuary in flight.

And like small children, too, they were lost in such a situation. They needed help of a kind that only he could give — want it or not. Only he was equipped from experience and with a weapon that would enable him to stand in the way of the outlaws. The Hebrenites must accept that truth.

He had no choice. He saw that now. He could not just ride on — hell, he still had to corner Bobby Joe and get back his belt buckle.

Keeping well down, he started for the partly buried sod shanty. Figures in the pale light at the rear of the blacksmith shop caught his attention, halted him. Three men were standing motionless, as if waiting. . . . And then a fourth running toward them from the adjoining feed storage warehouse.

Starbuck straightened as anxiety gripped him. What was Kilrain up to? The answer came suddenly. A spurt of fire brightened the alleyway. An oath ripped from Shawn's throat as understanding came to him. The outlaws had put a torch to the warehouse — and inside were Jaboe McIntyre and his family.

☆ 18 ☆

A woman was screaming into the night. Shawn saw a man dart into the alley behind the burning building, recognized the lean figure of McIntyre. He was carrying a child. Placing the youngster on the ground a safe distance from the flames, he wheeled, rushed back into the thickening clouds of smoke.

Starbuck, forgetting the presence of the outlaws, hurried across the open field to the blazing structure. Reaching there, he started to enter, and suddenly remembering, cast a quick glance to the luridly lit area where Kilrain and the others were standing. The outlaws had turned, were walking away, seemingly having no interest in him and none whatever in the doomed warehouse. Puzzled, he went on.

He had thought it was simply a way to draw him into the open, permit them to have it out with him. Instead— he shook his head as he dashed through the open doorway into the heat-filled interior of McIntyre's quarters, unable to understand. They had something else in mind, that was certain — some sort of plan that would enable them to gain the upper hand in a simpler, safer manner.

All thoughts were swept from his mind in that next instant. McIntyre, with two more children, one under each arm, sweat and soot streaking his face, beard singed, stumbled into him as he emerged from the choking pall.

He saw Starbuck, hauled up in surprise. His eyes narrowed, and then he bucked his chin at an adjoining doorway.

"In there — my wife! Make her come out!"

Shawn pushed by the agitated man, fought his way through the dense haze into the adjacent room. He could see a vague shape moving frantically about, gathering clothing, pieces of furniture, and other articles, piling all haphazardly onto a bed that had begun to smoulder. He crossed to her, seized her by the arm.

"Get out of here!" he yelled above the crackling of the flames. "Whole place is going up!"

She turned a shocked face to him, jerked free. "Our things — from home. . . . Got to save them —"

Starbuck stepped to the bed. Knocking aside the bulky pieces of furniture, he gathered up the corners of the bedspread, pulled it into a bulging bundle. Throwing it over his shoulder, he held it with his right hand, gripped the woman with his left. Whirling her about, he propelled her through the doorway and toward the building's rear exit.

The heat was intense. Flames had cut through the plank wall, dried by countless days of blistering sun, were licking hungrily at the ceiling. McIntyre, a rag tied over his nose and mouth, loomed up again in the smothering fog.

"Go back!" Starbuck shouted, pushing the woman at him. "Too late for anything else."

Jaboe bobbed his head, threw an arm about his wife, forced her into the open.

Shawn followed, trailed them through the bank of pungent smoke to where the Hebrenite had deposited the children, and dropped the bedcover bundle near them. Several of the Family had come from hiding, were standing by, some comforting the McIntyres, others simply watching the building's destruction with expressionless faces.

The flames mounted to their peak quickly, were spearing the night sky with darting yellow tongues. Now and then a sharp crackling and an occasional explosion sounded inside the structure, and showers of sparks would spurt into the duller glow as something combustible burst into flames.

The flames were beginning to lower, to die out, and the charred outlines of the gutted structure with its jagged, smouldering walls showed through the thinning banks of smoke. A few of the onlookers, curiously silent through it all, were fading off, heading back for their quarters. There were hardly any expressions of sympathy for the McIntyres, Shawn noted, just a mute acquiescence to the loss.

"You'll be putting up at the inn."

Starbuck recognized Oram Grey's modulated

voice. He wheeled, having been unaware of the man's presence, saw him speaking with Jaboe McIntyre. In him also was the same unruffled acceptance of the calamity.

McIntyre nodded, eyes on the building that had served as home as well as for the Family's storage depot. Fire yet glowed in the interior where sacks of grain sizzled and steamed hotly as in the crater of a seething volcano.

"Seed's all lost, Oram," he murmured. "Never saved a single, solitary cupful."

The Hebrenite leader shifted his moody eyes to the smoking ruin. "We can grow more — and a new house can be built in which to store it. Only wood and grain has been destroyed — not our will to do."

McIntyre said, "True," and moved over to where his family huddled with their possessions.

Shawn stepped up, took the blanket bundle, again slung it over his shoulder. McIntyre gave him a noncommittal glance, gathered two of the children to him.

"Bring little Aaron, mother," he said to his wife, and started through the smoke-filled darkness for the rear of the hotel.

Wordless, the woman reached for the hand of the third child, and moved to follow her husband. Starbuck, trailing last of all, looked to the side, again wondered about the outlaws.

They were not to be seen anywhere along the alley, but as he drew near the hotel, and the old

Mason house at the end of the street where they quartered became visible, he could see light in the window and shadowy figures moving about inside.

They had returned to the shack, had settled down. Again he wondered what Con Kilrain had in mind. That he and the others were forgetting his presence, ignoring the fact that he had killed Rollie Lister, and calling it quits was an impossibility; with them it took blood to square up for blood.

McIntyre led the way up to the hotel's stairs, stepping around the body of the dead outlaw, and entered the building. Simon Pierce was waiting inside the door. Beyond him stood Patience, several articles of night clothing draped over an arm. Farther on Starbuck caught sight of Hetty and Esther. Evidently the younger girl had overcome her reluctance to face her parents. Their relief at seeing him was apparent.

"Room's ready for you," Pierce said, smiling at the soot-and-smoke-marked couple. "You want to wash up, there's water in the tub and pitcher."

"I've got some things here you might need," Patience added.

"Thanking you kindly," McIntyre replied, "but we saved a little — what we're wearing and a few things Mercy was able to grab. . . . Would like some salve. There's a few burns."

Patience nodded, hurried off into another part of the building. Jaboe, releasing his grip on the hands of the children, wheeled, took the bundle from Shawn, and shepherding his family before him, steered them into the room.

Pausing in the doorway, he looked back at Starbuck. His smeared face, showing angry red in spots where live sparks had fallen upon him, was withdrawn, almost hating.

"Obliged to you for helping, but I'm remembering that because of you —"

"Don't give me that!" Shawn cut in, anger and impatience finally getting the best of him. "Was those outlaws who started it. Saw them, only it was too late to do anything about it."

"He's not to be blamed, Jaboe," Pierce said in a calming voice. "He was only the tool, a part of a plan — one beyond our understanding."

"Plan!" Starbuck shouted the word. "What's the matter with you people? That fire was set by Con Kilrain and his bunch. They're taking you — this whole town — over, saddle, cinch, and singletree, and you do nothing about it, just stand around and let them get away with it. They'll have —"

"It's all according to the way it is to be," Pierce murmured.

Shawn wagged his head. "Don't mean to dispute your beliefs, but there's only one reason for that fire — Kilrain. He's got something in mind."

Simon studied him briefly, eyed the bandanna bandage still encircling his head. Then, "That

159

makes no sense. Why would they do it of their own wish? A greater wisdom prompted —"

"You can expect them to be doing a lot of things like this before they're through," Starbuck broke in.

"Perhaps —"

"We are but a part of a single plan — such is what we believe," Oram Grey said.

Shawn pivoted. The leader of the Family had come up the back steps unheard and unnoticed, was standing in the open doorway.

"We do not question, we simply accept."

Starbuck sighed, lifted his arms, let them fall to his sides in resignation. "You've got a strange way of looking at things. You're telling me that Kilrain and his crowd can go right ahead, do anything they like, and you'll let them do it?"

"Our answer to oppression is to remove ourselves from it, not oppose or attempt to fight it. To do so gains nothing. It serves only to create greater contention that must be coped with later. Violence leads only to more violence, and each time it grows. . . . If a man turns his back upon such, it is then brought to an end, and doors to future trouble are closed."

Shawn remained silent for a time. Finally, "Guess I can understand some of your reasoning but I can't say I agree with it. And it's sure your right to live anyway you want — only this time you're up against something different. Your ideas won't work."

Oram Grey stalked into the room, a tall, lean sober-faced figure. His black eyes peered out from beneath their thick brows with a steady piercing intent.

"There can be no reason why it will not. Always it has been the answer."

Grey was making no reference in any way to the meeting that had taken place between them that previous night during which he had requested Shawn's aid in delivering the settlement from the outlaws. Apparently he had undergone a change of view — or still did not wish his followers to know that he broke the principal tenet of their faith. . . . If that was the way he wanted it, Shawn decided, then he would respect that silence.

"They won't let you pull out — move on — if that's what you've got figured as the answer."

Simon Pierce nodded hesitantly. "They stopped him, Oram — this morning. Left him for dead."

It was difficult to think Grey was unaware of the outlaws' determination to keep the valley a locked vault, and Shawn wondered if the Hebrenite leader didn't actually realize it but, for the sake of his people, refused to admit it.

"Why would they object? Everything would be left to them — supplies, houses, our crops. We'd ask only permission to go in peace."

"One mighty big reason," Starbuck said. "They don't want the location of the valley known."

"We'd not tell. This we would promise, on our word —"

"You — there inside the hotel! Come out on the porch. Got some talking to do!"

It was Con Kilrain's harsh voice.

☆ 19 ☆

A small cry broke from Hetty's lips. "It's the outlaws! They've come to —"

Oram Grey lifted a broad hand for silence, smiled comfortingly at her. "Don't be afraid. There's no cause for alarm. They only want to talk."

He moved by Shawn, aiming for the lobby. Starbuck caught at his arm. "Do your talking from the inside. You can't trust —"

"There's no reason to fear," Grey insisted.

"No reason! What does it take to make you realize that you're dealing with killers?"

"Killers? Perhaps, but he said he wanted to talk. . . . He has a plan."

"Hell!" Starbuck exploded in disgust, and then lowered his head apologetically to the women standing nearby. "Only plan Con Kilrain's got is one to take over everything around here — and he'll stop at nothing to do it."

"You — inside! Coming out or am I coming in?"

Simon Pierce stepped up to Oram's side. "I'll stand with you, Elder," he said.

Shawn sighed wearily, released his grip on

the man's arm. He brushed at the sweat on his brow. "All right, have it your way. But keep remembering this, you can't trust any of that bunch out there — not one. They're different from any you've ever come up against. They're killers who'll die before they'll let themselves be captured and sent back to that army prison — and they'll do their figuring accordingly. Be smart — don't take any chances."

"How about it, you sodbusters?"

Shawn recognized Bobby Joe's voice, hard-edged and pressing.

At once Oram Grey, with Pierce at his shoulder, entered the lobby and crossed to the entrance. The two men paused there briefly, as if girding themselves for battle, then stepped out onto the gallery.

Starbuck, moving fast but careful to keep out of sight, slipped in close to the window adjacent to the doorway. Cautiously he drew back the edge of the curtain.

Kilrain and Bobby Joe Grant were in the center of the street. A dozen strides to their left was Abe Norvel. The outlaw called Shep had stationed himself a similar distance to the right. They were not permitting themselves to collect in one group.

"I'm Oram Grey — the Senior Elder —"

"I don't give a hoot and a damn who you are, grandpa," Kilrain said in a jeering tone. "What I've got to say goes for everybody in this dump."

Starbuck, hand resting on the butt of his pistol, felt fingers grip his wrist. He glanced around. Hetty was standing beside him looking up into his face. Her features were strained, eyes filled with concern.

"Shawn — I'm afraid — for pa."

He nodded. "They would've shown more sense if they'd done their talking from in here."

"I know. I heard what you told them. But they don't believe in fear — or in not trusting."

"Man walks into a den of rattlesnakes, trust's not much protection. I'll watch sharp, try to keep something from happening to them."

"That fire," Kilrain was saying, his words pitched to carry the length of the street to those he could not see but knew were listening as well as to the pair standing on the gallery, "we set it."

Oram Grey's reply was calm. "We know that. You were seen."

The outlaw paused, stared at the older men. He turned his head, muttered something to Bobby Joe, who laughed. Moonlight glinted softly off the buckle of the belt he was wearing. *My belt,* Starbuck thought, and felt the stir of anger. It was an insult to the memory of old Hiram.

"Reckon you've been told this already by my boys," Kilrain continued, "but I'll tell you again, sort of make it official. I'm taking over the place, making it my headquarters."

The men on the porch remained silent,

simply waited, two bent, graying figures, meek and pitiful.

"You folks do what you're told and we'll get along fine. Give me trouble and you'll wish to God you'd never been born!"

"What do you expect of us?" Oram asked.

"Grub — plenty of it, along with everything else it'll take to keep us going." He hesitated again as Bobby Joe made a remark, laughed, and added, "Includes women and whiskey."

"There's no liquor here —"

"You've got plenty of grain. You can make it. 'Til then, reckon we can bring in our drinking — you just see to the rest."

Oram Grey began to shake his head slowly. He took a step forward. "We can't agree to that," he stated clearly. "We'd be slaves."

"Yeh, guess you would."

"Then we'll leave. We'll take our people and move on. The valley will be yours to do with as you wish."

"Like hell you'll leave! Nobody moves out of here without my say-so! You think I want the law knowing where I'm holed up?"

"We'll not speak of it. You'll have our word."

"Word — that don't mean a goddamn thing to me, grandpa! I want you here — every last one of you. Going to need you to look after us, keep us eating and sleeping and such —"

"So's we can grow fat and rich," Bobby Joe volunteered.

"That's right."

Oram Grey wagged his head stubbornly. "No, we can't do it. We won't. . . . We'll leave — somehow."

The slap of a pistol shot shattered the hush. Splinters flew from the plank flooring at Grey's feet. Both men jumped back, Oram's hat coming off in the process and rolling crazily along on its brim.

"I ain't just jawin' to hear myself," Kilrain said in a dead cold voice. "You damn well better get that in your head right now! There ain't none of you pulling out — and when the rest of your tribe gets back from selling them cattle, they'll pitch right in and help with the rest of you. . . . I'll be taking the cash they got, too. . . . You won't be needing any."

"We'll not stay — be made slaves," Oram Grey insisted quietly.

"Reckon you will, grandpa. This here's the place where you'll live and you'll die — one way or another. And any time one of your bunch gets out of line, you can figure on paying for it plenty. Like that there fire we set tonight. Was just a little sample."

In the pale moonlight Oram's white hair looked to be pure silver. He drew himself up to his full height. "We won't stay," he said again. "We were born free, and we'll die free — not as slaves —"

The pistol in Con Kilrain's hand flared again, hurled its sound into the night. Oram Grey staggered, a look of pained surprise on his thin

167

face as he clutched at his chest. Slowly he began to sink. Somewhere inside the hotel a woman began to sob.

Starbuck, a wild anger lashing at him, jerked away from the window. Pistol in hand, he lunged for the door. Hetty threw herself upon him, pressed him back.

"No! It'll only mean more killing — you, pa, some of the rest of us!"

Shawn hesitated. She was right, of course. He might cut down Kilrain, possibly even Bobby Joe, but Norvel and Shep, off to opposite sides, would drop him quickly — along with anyone else who happened to be in the general line of fire. . . . Besides, as long as the outlaws were unaware of his whereabouts, he had the upper hand and could do much more good.

"Reckon you all savvy now what I'm saying, and that I ain't just horsing you around."

Con Kilrain's irritating voice was an abrasion rubbing Starbuck raw. Again at the window he watched the outlaw calmly rod the empty cartridges from his weapon.

Simon Pierce, kneeling next to Grey's crumpled shape, stared at Kilrain.

"You've killed him. . . . He's dead."

"Sure he's dead. What I aimed at him being. No big loss no-how. Old man like him ain't good for nothing — same as a one-armed cripple. . . . And he had himself a loose jaw. Would've been handing me back a lot of lip all the time.

"Now, they's no need for any more of this. I've laid the law down to you. Follow it and you'll live peaceable and there'll be no trouble. . . . That's part of what I'm here to tell you. The next thing's —"

"It all right if I get some help, take him inside?" Pierce interrupted, coming to his feet.

"Nope, you stand right where you are, mister. He ain't going nowhere shape he's in. When I'm done talking, then you can lug him off to the boneyard and plant him. Take that other'n laying out back of the place, too.

"Now, that next thing I was talking about — you're hiding a drifter — jasper that shot one of my boys. I want him. Where is he?"

Simon Pierce stood mute.

"Well, no sweat. Know he's around somewheres — and I ain't wasting no more time or men digging him up. Some of your bunch is covering him and I'm giving you orders here and now to roust him out and hand him over. Hear?"

"Could be he's gone," Pierce said. "Know he was planning to ride —"

"He ain't gone. We just seen him a bit ago, and he ain't had a chance to leave town — so don't go lying to me about it. Now, you've got 'til sunup to hand him over. I want him coming right out that there door behind you. First he's to throw that gun he's got into the street. Then he's to follow it. Savvy?"

Simon nodded woodenly.

169

"Good. . . . If you don't dig him up, then I'm putting a torch to the church. If that don't do it, the store'll be next — and I'll keep right on building bonfires until you show some sense and march him out here. Clear?"

"Clear," Simon Pierce said in a low voice.

"It better be." Kilrain hitched at his gun belt, bobbed his head decisively. "Come sunrise I'll be standing right here. . . . You sure better have him waiting for me."

☆ 20 ☆

Shawn understood now the strange actions of Kilrain and his men after the fire had started; they had made no effort to hunt him down, simply figured to avoid the risk of a shoot-out and the possible death of another of their members by ignoring him. It was easier and safer to force the people of the valley to hand him over.

Silent, he watched the outlaws fade back into the shadows, and then again started for the porch. It was Patience who stopped him this time.

"They might see you and —" She could not say the words. "We'll look after him," she finished and, followed by Jaboe McIntyre and another man of the valley, stepped out onto the starlit gallery. Moments later they reappeared, the two men carrying Oram's body between them, Simon and Patience walking alongside.

"That room off the hall," the woman said in a businesslike voice as they crossed the lobby, "we'll use it."

Other members of the Family, witnessing the murder from their quarters or being advised of it, began to arrive. They came in quietly, filed into the bedroom where Oram Grey was laid.

They had their last look at the stilled sunken face, now reflecting the great age of the man, and moved on into the larger area of the hotel's lobby where they stood about in hushed groups.

Patience produced a thick white blanket, and assisted by Hetty and some of the women, began to prepare a shroud. A coffin would not be necessary, the girl told Shawn when he offered to help in the construction of such; the Hebrenites believed the mortal remains of their departed should be permitted to return to dust as speedily as possible.

In the dim lobby, with the remaining Elders and various members of the sect, Starbuck felt apart — a stranger among passive people with ways and customs that were odd to him. He was the outsider, the unbeliever, and from the hastily averted glances he caught time and again when he looked around, he realized they felt he was the cause of their tribulations — at fault for the death of Oram Grey.

He supposed he was to some extent. However, if he hadn't stumbled onto the valley and the Hebrenite village, Con Kilrain and his renegades would still have taken over and forced their will upon the inhabitants. He hadn't been the cause of their coming; he hadn't led them there; his presence had only brought matters to a head sooner.

Perhaps there would have been no killing. That was a question that now could never be answered. But one thing was certain in Shawn's mind, Oram Grey would have defied Con Kilrain regardless; he was a brave man, determined never to allow his people to become slaves.

However, that thin dividing line that separated cause and fault was of no interest to Starbuck. His mind was now filled with thoughts of the crisis that would come with the rising of the sun. He drifted slowly to the window, looked out into the deserted street. Moonlight had strengthened, mingled with the glow of stars, and now lay a soft, pale radiance — gentle and friendly — over all. But death had walked there in that mellowness — and would do so again.

"Shawn —"

He turned to face Esther Grey. He had noted her earlier standing aside from the others, as did he; she was one of the Family, tolerated but shunned and ignored. If it disturbed her, it did not show. In her hands she held a strip of cloth, a bandage. There was a smear of medicine of some sort on it. Removing his hat, he bent forward slightly, allowed her to replace the stained bandanna.

"I'm sorry for the way this is turning out," she murmured when she had finished.

He shrugged. "No need. Cards don't always fall like you'd want them to."

"What will you do?"

He hesitated for a long breath, said, "Only

thing I can, play out the hand."

"That's foolishness. . . . You could leave tonight. I'll get you a horse — manage it somehow."

Starbuck gave her a wry smile. "Still got to get back my gear," he said. His face sobered. "You realize what Kilrain and his bunch would do to all of you if I ran out?"

"Perhaps nothing — there's no way of really knowing. If they did take it out on the Family, it would be no more than what they deserved."

He shrugged. What Esther suggested would be fine for him, but it would spell the worst kind of trouble for the Hebrenites; and he couldn't save himself at the expense of Oram Grey's people.

"We'll see," he murmured. "Could be it'll all work out better than we think."

A huddle being engaged in by Pierce, McIntyre, Micah Jones, Vinsent, and another bearded individual broke up suddenly.

Esther frowned, said, "They've made up their minds. I hope they plan to help you."

"Could use a bit, sure enough," Shawn replied and turned to meet Simon.

"We've talked," Pierce said. "We've decided that something must be done before more blood is spilled."

Starbuck waited in silence.

"We've agreed that you should leave here."

McIntyre nodded. "We'll get you a horse and provide supplies, then we'll take you to a place west of here where you can get out of the valley. Only a few of us know the trail — it leads up to a pass. It's hard to find, hard to travel, but if a man'll lead his animal —"

Shawn had folded his arms across his chest, was shaking his head slowly. "Expect you'd best go back and do some more talking. It's plain you don't understand what'll happen around here if you help me get away."

"We don't want no more killings," Micah Jones said. "If it has to be put blunt — we're telling you to leave."

"You think my going will stop their killing?"

"If you're gone, there'll be no reason."

"Fooling yourself," Starbuck cut in impatiently. "What Kilrain sure doesn't want is for me — or anybody — to ride out. You heard him say that."

"He's after you for shooting his man."

"Part of it — but that's not the big thing. He has to be sure nobody gets out of here and tells the law or the army where he's hiding — and spoils a good thing for him."

"But if you gave your word — or we did —"

"None of you seem to realize what Kilrain and the others can do — and will! Shooting down a man in cold blood means nothing to them. You saw that tonight — right out there on the porch."

"We don't aim to put up any resistance, give them cause —"

"You'll be giving them plenty of cause if you

175

don't produce me in the morning. They don't respect your beliefs or your bravery when you stand up to them without a gun. They laugh at you, figure you for a fool — and grab the advantage. . . . Can't you see you're throwing your lives away?"

Ezrah Vinsent stirred indifferently. "No worse than meeting them with a gun and dying from one of their bullets. Dead's dead."

"Won't deny that but at least you've not let them trample you into the dirt like you were a weed or a bug of some sort."

"We've always been peaceable folk, avoiding violence, even at the expense of our land," Pierce said slowly.

"Know that — and you're going to keep on paying that price until there's none of you left — which won't be long. You can't go on believing in that. Might've worked a hundred years ago, maybe even fifty, but it won't work now.

"Thing is, the world can get along without you, but nowadays you can't get along without the world. It's over there, the other side of the hill, whether you want to admit it or not. That's why you're losing your sons and your daughters. They can see it and they're pulling out because they know the old ideas won't work anymore.

"Be a real fine thing if it would. A man's entitled to peace, to live and work and think the way he likes. But there're always the Kilrains and the Bobby Joes and such who'll come in, take what they want by force unless somebody stops them."

Frustrated by the older men's bland indifference, by his failure to get through to them, make them understand, angry at himself for becoming involved and allowing himself to get so worked up, Starbuck wheeled, strode to the window, again looked out into the night.

There was a stillness in the crowded, stuffy room when Starbuck finished. A lamp on one of the tables began to sputter. An elderly woman in a solid black dress turned hastily, snuffed out the flickering flame.

Micah Jones shifted heavily. "It'd be wrong for us to use violence. Keep telling you that, Starbuck — and we plain won't allow it! Oram believed in that, same as did all the Senior Elders before him, and our people, too. We ain't no different in our believing."

Shawn came back around slowly, considered the lowered, intent features of the men before him. He could tell them their leader, facing up to reality, had visited him in the night, sought to have him remove the outlaw threat from their midst. Oram Grey was dead and words could not hurt him.

But they could destroy the memory of the man and all that his followers thought he stood for. To tell them that Oram Grey in desperation had advocated violence in its strongest form would be cruel — although such revelation could be the one factor that would swing them to his way of thinking. . . . But he'd not do it; he'd find a means other than by indicting a fine old gentleman who could not now explain or defend his actions.

"Not asking any of you, personally, to take a hand — just that you understand what I've got to do and not interfere."

Hetty looked up at him quickly, a worried frown on her young face. "You can't fight them alone — not all four of them!"

"There's only one gun. I took it off Lister's body because I've no cartridges for my own. Even if there was someone willing, there'd be no weapon to use."

"But you can't do it by yourself! It would be suicide!" Impulsively Hetty wheeled, faced her father and the others in the room. "You can't let him do it alone! You've got to help, somehow! Does he have to get down on his knees, beg you to let him throw away his life to save yours?"

Starbuck laid a hand on the girl's shoulder, brought her around gently. "Best this be left to me. I've been up this trail before, know what I'm bucking."

"But, by yourself — alone — how —"

Shawn glanced to the rear of the lobby. Through the open door he could see men carrying in Rollie Lister. The women were preparing a shroud for him, too, it appeared. His gaze returned to the immediate room, drifted over the faces of those gathered there. A dozen or so children were present — boys and girls in their early teens, or not quite to that point. They were watching him and their elders closely, eyes betraying the doubt and confusion that gripped their minds.

"Don't know that myself — yet," he said to Hetty, and then swung to Simon Pierce. "Let's get it settled. Need to know where I am. Realize there's enough of you to throw a rope around me, put me on a horse, and take me out of the valley if you're of a mind to. Or you can hand me over to Kilrain. Want the answer now because sunup's going to be here before we know it."

Again a silence fell over the room. Simon adjusted his empty sleeve, then nervously scrubbed at his chin. He touched Micah Jones and the others with a long glance, looked at Shawn.

"You saying you'd stand up to those outlaws by yourself, whether we want it or not?"

"Only thing I can do."

Again Pierce's gaze swept his fellow Elders, this time as if seeking confirmation. "All right, let it be your way. We'll not interfere."

"And you'll not help either!" Hetty cried, whirling on her father. "You'll just sit back, let him go out there and die! I'm ashamed of that — of what you are — of what we all are! And if this is the way I'm supposed to think and the sort of life I've been raised to live — I don't want any part of it. . . . I'll take the world Shawn comes from."

Eyes flashing, cheeks glowing, Hetty stepped in close to Starbuck, turned her face to him. "Maybe I won't have any weapon when you step out there into the street, but I'll be with you. . . . I want you to know there's one person in this valley who realizes what you're doing and's not afraid to die with you."

☆ 21 ☆

A full hour before first light Starbuck eased himself out of the hotel's rear entrance. Sticking to the shadows, he crossed to the barn and thence to the brush below the settlement. He knew it was probably a waste of time but he felt the need to see if Kilrain and his partners were so sure of themselves that they would throw caution to the wind and spend the night in their usual quarters.

He didn't hold out much hope for such; the outlaw — certain of his ground insofar as the Hebrenites were concerned after demonstrating his ruthlessness by shooting down Oram Grey and burning the feed warehouse — was still no fool. There remained one threat to the empire he was hoping to build — a man with a gun who could meet him on even terms, perhaps kill him. He'd run no risk of that coming to pass but maintain a wariness until the threat was removed.

Nevertheless, Shawn was looking into all possibilities. He could be misjudging Con Kilrain's intelligence, and because he needed an edge, he was investigating all angles. He was not fooling anybody, much less himself, into thinking he could go up against four hardened killers and come out unscathed. The only way he could come out of such an encounter alive was by first seeking out an advantage, and then making the most of it.

Hunkered in the rabbit brush and sage, he studied the old Mason place. The horses were gone from the hitchrack, stabled in the adjoining shack, he assumed. A lamp burned in the parlor, threw a weak yellow glow against the walls and through the windows and open doorways.

An invitation, Shawn thought, beckoning to him, asking him to move in close and let one of the outlaws — whichever one had been posted to watch — put a bullet in his head and thus solve the problem even before dawn broke. He grinned. *No dice, Kilrain. . . . I'm not that big a sucker.*

Glancing to the east to be certain there was still ample time, he continued south until he was well below the settlement, and there crossed over, dropping into an arroyo — the same used that preceding day when he had returned from his fruitless attempt to leave the valley with Esther and Hetty.

Kilrain could be using the same wash, employing it as a place, somewhat apart from the houses and buildings, from which to keep an eye on all that went on. With that in mind, Shawn continued up the arroyo but now with greater care.

Approaching the first bend, which lay directly behind the Mason place and its adjacent neighbors, he drew in close to the bank, and straining to see in the poor light, halted.

No one was in the arroyo as far as he could tell. He shifted his attention to the outlaws' quarters. The lamp in the parlor reached through the connecting entries, illuminated the kitchen and the back bedroom where Hetty had been held captive. Clearly, both were empty.

He had guessed right about Con Kilrain. The outlaw was taking no chance on being surprised by his intended victim slipping in and catching him and his friends asleep. Indeed, the lighted but vacant quarters indicated he sought the exact opposite.

They could be holed up most anywhere in the settlement or along its fringes, Shawn realized, beginning a careful backtrack. There was no sense in trying to ferret them out. Best he occupy himself in the time that remained by coming up with a plan to meet Kilrain's demands — and still stay alive.

Back at the rear of the hotel, he started to mount the steps, halted when a figure arose from the half dark at the side of the steps. His hand dropped swiftly to the gun at his side, fell away when he saw that it was Esther.

She came forward to meet him, features serious, worried. "I've been waiting for you."

"Something wrong?"

She shook her head. "Nothing more than usual. I'm going to meet Abe. . . . I don't know

183

where he is, but he'll see me and come to me. . . . I just wanted to say thank you and tell you that I hope things come out all right."

He studied her thoughtfully. "Guess you know one of us has to lose. They may get me — and I'll have to kill Abe if he gets in front of my gun."

"I know," she murmured in a lost voice. "I only wish I could do something — help —"

"Obliged for the thought. Want to say I'm sorry, too, we didn't get through that gate first try. At least you'd be out of it."

"And you —"

He nodded. "Reckon so." But he wasn't at all sure. The fact that he had left the Hebrenites in the clutches of the outlaws would have weighed heavily on his mind, and the probability that he would have turned back once he had the two women safely away was strong. "Well, got to start figuring what I'll do. . . . Good luck if I don't see you again."

"Good luck to you," Esther said, and moved on.

Starbuck climbed the steps, entered quietly, and made his way to the lobby. He could hear voices in the kitchen beyond the dining room, guessed Simon Pierce and the Elders were still up and hashing over their problems. Or perhaps they were just waiting for sunrise. It would be like riding out the minutes before an execution.

Crossing the deserted lobby, he took up one

184

of the straight-backed chairs, placed it at the window. Drawing back the curtain, he sat down. He had waited at the same point earlier, had listened to Con Kilrain deliver his ultimatum, had watched him gun down Oram Grey. It was an excellent position from which to view the area immediately in front of the hotel — but that was of little use to him. He should be in the street, not looking into it when the moment of confrontation came.

He tried to figure how Kilrain would set up his deathtrap. All four of the outlaws would not be in a single group — he was positive of that. Such would place them in a dangerous situation and Con had already proven he was taking no unnecessary risks.

Likely Kilrain would be the lone representative standing in front of the hotel. Bobby Joe Grant, Shep, and Abe Norvel would be covering him from strategic positions elsewhere along the way, just in the event matters didn't work out exactly as anticipated, and their would-be victim came out of the doorway shooting.

He glanced again to the horizon in the east. A pearl glow was making itself visible above the dark hills, extending the first hint of a new day. A wry thought entered his mind; he guessed he was pinning on Oram Grey's paper star after all.

His shoulders lifted, fell resignedly. Reaching down he drew his pistol — Rollie Lister's actually — absently checked the loads. He had a cartridge in each of the six openings of the cylinder, a practice to which he did not ordinarily subscribe, but again he felt it wise under the circumstances. That extra bullet could be the one to save his life.

His own weapon, useless without bullets, was thrust into his waistband. He would feel more comfortable with it on his hip and in his hand when the time came to make use of a weapon, but there was no way to make that possible. He might as well leave it there in the lobby, relieve himself of that much excess weight . . . Unless . . . Starbuck frowned, considered the heavy forty-five through half-closed eyes. . . . Maybe —

A sound behind him brought him around. It was Hetty. She had been in the kitchen with the others. He gave her a short smile.

"I didn't hear you come back in," she said, her voice faintly accusing, as she drew up a chair next to his. "Did you find out anything?"

He shrugged. "Like I figured, they weren't fools enough to stay in the Mason shack. Did have it all set up for me — lamps lit and all."

"Are you going to try and find them?"

"Nope. . . . Good rule at a time like this is to let the man looking for you do the hunting." He paused, jerked his thumb toward the kitchen. "Been quite a meeting. Lasted the whole night."

Hetty sighed. "Just talking — and waiting.

186

They won't do anything to help you. Sad part of it is they wouldn't know how if they wanted to." She turned her eyes to the window. The vague pearl band was now a bright flare reaching up into the sky. "Shawn — it won't be long until the sun's up."

"Not long," he agreed, making no issue of it before her.

She sighed deeply. "You weren't depending on them were you?"

"No."

Her voice was wooden, hopeless in its quality. "Have you thought of a way — a plan that'll —"

"Keep me from getting killed? Not yet. Not much I can do until I see how Kilrain aims to handle it. He'll scatter his bunch, can depend on that. Just where's the important thing to me. Once I know that, I can go from there. Did get an idea about that part."

The fan of pearl was showing streaks of color. All along the street the shadows were thinning and definition was returning to the objects turned mysterious and unfamiliar by the night.

Hetty was staring at him. "An idea — can I help with it?"

"Could be, but I'll not run the risk of you getting yourself hurt. Important you stay inside the hotel out of danger."

"I will, but it really doesn't matter. Nothing does, it seems. I guess I've sort of grown up during the night."

"We all have, probably. . . . Something like

187

this can do it — can make you realize how little some things count and how much other things do."

Chair legs scraped against the kitchen floor. A door opened somewhere allowing a light wind to breeze through the hotel, sweep clean the mustiness stagnating in the lobby. Somewhere nearby an overzealous rooster crowed shakily.

Starbuck rose, glanced once again to the east. He was frowning, torn between the need to put the plan that had come into his mind into effect, and the wisdom of forgetting it.

Still undecided, because it involved Hetty, he said, "Want to get outside, be there when the time comes."

Hetty got to her feet, relief easing some of the tautness in her face. "Then you're not going to just walk out the door — let him shoot —"

"Not about to. He'll not take me that easy."

"But if you don't —"

"Think I've got a way around it. Just came to me. I'll need your help but it's no deal unless I've got your promise to stay inside — not leave this lobby."

The girl nodded eagerly. "I'll promise, Shawn. What do you want me to do?"

"Kilrain's orders were for me to throw my gun out into the street," he said, taking the useless forty-five and handing it to her. "Then I'm to step out onto the porch. What I want you to do is stand inside the door. When he hollers for

188

me to do it, count ten and toss out the gun. . . . You've got to be sure he doesn't see that you're the one doing it."

"I understand. You want him to think it's you inside."

"That's the idea."

"But when you don't show yourself —"

"Those few moments I'll gain after you throw out my gun are all I'll need. Bobby Joe and the others will have their sights lined up on the door. When they see the gun hit the street, they'll figure there's no danger of me trying to shoot my way out, and come out from where Kilrain's got them hiding. . . . And I'll be out there watching and waiting for that."

Hetty clasped the heavy weapon in her two hands, faced him, eyes dark and deeply worried. "It sounds all right — but I'm still afraid for you."

"Don't be. A little edge like that's all a man needs. Fact is, I've been in worse tights — and luck's been running with me. Expect it'll keep right on."

She nodded vigorously as if to convince herself. "I know it will, and I'll pray for you, Shawn, pray that you'll not get hurt and that you'll come back to me. Then we can go away — together — leave all this behind and —"

He reached out, laid a finger upon her lips, stilled the words. "No," he said in a low, firm voice. "Not together, Hetty. It's not for me — the kind of life you're looking for and deserve.

I've a brother to find, one I've been hunting for a long time. I can't quit until the job's done. . . . After that — maybe —"

She was utterly silent, features dark, her eyes filled with the dullness of rejection. And then abruptly she turned, dropped the pistol onto the chair. Reaching up, she put her arms about his neck, and drawing him down, kissed him hurriedly.

"I'll still pray," she murmured, and taking up the pistol again, moved toward the door.

☆ 22 ☆

Shawn let himself out the rear of the hotel with caution. Light was now spreading over the land and there was the possibility that Con Kilrain had posted one of his men to cover that exit.

Taking full advantage of the shadows, the bin where cut wood was stacked, and the walls of an extending closet, he ignored the steps and dropped to the ground from the landing. Wheeling at once, he cut south, followed a course much the same as he had taken earlier when he had gone to have his look at the outlaws' quarters.

He'd make his play from there. What was more logical than to hide himself in the one place where he knew absolutely none of the gang would be? It made good sense to him, and moving with hurried care, he skirted the settlement, reached the arroyo, and traveling its sandy track, came to where he was opposite the Mason shack and its adjacent decaying companions.

As before there was no way he could tell if any of the men were inside, and he could not risk finding out. He'd simply have to lie low until proceedings began and he had some in-

191

kling of where the outlaws were — then do what appeared to be the most effective thing.

Hunched in the wash, shoulders against the wall, he watched the flare in the east change slowly into long fingers of salmon and rose, thence to a sheet of purest gold, and finally, as the rim of the sun peeped over the ragged hills, to a white hot blue.

In that same instant he heard Con Kilrain's voice break the hush that lay over the settlement. Kilrain was making good use of the dramatic, knowing his precise punctuality would serve to impress the Hebrenites more firmly as to the inflexibility of his will.

"All right, drifter — time's come."

The sound of the outlaw chief's voice startled a dog, set the animal to barking furiously.

"Don't go getting no cute ideas now. You ain't got a chance in hell — 'cause there's four guns covering you."

Shawn delayed no further. The outlaws, wherever they were, would have their attention focused on the hotel's doorway. Rising, he vaulted over the edge of the arroyo, raced to the back of the Mason place. Darting through the rear entrance, he crossed to the front, drew to a halt.

Crouched close to the door frame, he threw his glance up the street. Kilrain stood in approximately the same spot as he had that previous night. His thumbs were hooked in his belt, his legs were spraddled, and his crumpled broad-brimmed hat was pushed to the back of his head. The arrogance of the man was infuriating.

"You hear, drifter? Throw out your iron — now!"

Mentally Starbuck ticked off the count. Promptly at the beat of ten he saw the faint glitter of steel as his pistol arced from the hotel entrance, fell to the street in a spurt of dust.

"Fine. . . . Fine. You're playing it smart."

Shawn saw Bobby Joe then. The young outlaw had been standing at the far corner of the general store. At the surrendering of the pistol, he stepped into full view at the edge of the building's board landing. Motion across from him, at the forward end of the blacksmith shop, betrayed Shep's position.

Two of them — plus Kilrain, accounted for . . . Where was Abe Norvel?

Disturbed, realizing that with each passing second a part of the advantage he had managed to gain was being wiped out, Starbuck again searched the street for a sign of the missing outlaw. He should be to Kilrain's left; such would permit him to cover the lobby door from a different angle as well as guard his chief's flank. . . . He could be in one of the other shacks — the one at the end of the row. It would be nearest Kilrain.

He must know — positively. Norvel's bullet coming from an unexpected quarter could cost him his life. Grim, he turned, cut back through the rooms of the Mason place intending to cross over to the shack being used as a stable. If Abe wasn't hiding in there, it was almost a certainty he'd be in the third house.

Pressed by the urgency of fleeting time, he rushed through the doorway into the open — and froze. Directly in front of him was Norvel leading a horse. Beside the outlaw was Esther Grey, also walking her mount.

Starbuck's hand flashed down for the pistol on his hip. Norvel, knees bending slightly, went for his weapon.

"No — Shawn!" Esther cried, rushing in between them. "We're leaving —"

Starbuck, not removing his eyes from the man, base of his thumb hooked over the hammer of his pistol while the remainder of his big hand wrapped about the weapon preparatory to drawing and firing, rocked back gently. Kilrain's voice reached him from the street but he gave it no attention. . . . One thing at a time. . . .

"It's true!" Esther continued, her features taut with fear. "Abe's quit Kilrain — giving it up. . . . We're going away."

Norvel, holding also to his pistol, nodded slowly. "What we're doing," he murmured. "Can believe it or not."

"I'll be more apt to believe it when you take your hand off that gun," Starbuck said in a low voice.

In the tense hush Norvel shifted his eyes to

Esther. It was as if he needed reassuring. She nodded at once. Slowly then he let his arm fall away.

"Kilrain know about this?" Starbuck asked.

"No — we'd never get out of here alive if he did," Abe replied.

"Then best be on your way," Shawn said, and moved on, seeing the smile of relief and gratitude on the woman's lips. "Good luck."

"Same to you — friend," Norvel responded in a low voice.

". . . ain't waiting no longer —"

Kilrain's tone was angry. Shawn, turning into the narrow yard that separated the converted stable from the end shack, threw a glance over his shoulder. Esther and Abe Norvel had reached the lower section of the arroyo where they could no longer be seen from the settlement, were mounting. . . . He owed much to the yellow-haired woman; in persuading Norvel to break with the outlaws she had done him a great favor. . . . He was pleased to think that this time she'd make it out of the valley.

"Come out of there — hands over your head! Hear?"

Starbuck reached the front of the house, halted. Con Kilrain was in the open before him, easy to see, to cut down with a bullet. On beyond, Bobby Joe and Shep still held to their positions. Norvel, he supposed, had been stationed about where he now stood — except that he would be inside the shack.

"Goddammit — you'd better come out or I'm —"

"I'm here, Kilrain — right here!"

Cool, nerves tuned to razor sharpness, Shawn stepped into the street. He sent his first bullet into Shep, believing him to present the greatest threat because he was directly opposite and in position for a quick shot. He saw the outlaw buckle, start to fall, and jerked to one side — aware of a sudden loud commotion along the buildings.

It was a shattering racket of pounding and hammering that began to bounce back and forth between the building facades, echo discordantly, and quickly added to by the barking of a score of frightened dogs.

A distraction, pure and simple, calculated by Simon Pierce and the others to be no more, no less. Shawn knew instantly what was happening; the Hebrenites were helping after all, providing him with that breath of time he so badly needed to duck away, avoid the return bullets from the weapons of Bobby Joe Grant and Kilrain that he must expect. . . . And too, it could be they were demonstrating to the young ones of the sect that the outlaws provoked no fear in them.

Low, running hard, he dashed back along the area behind the shacks. He rounded the corner, crossed behind the last structure, and started for the street.

Con Kilrain was before him. He had anticipated Starbuck, was crouched, weapon leveled. Pure hatred distorted his dark face.

Shawn fired instinctively, spun half about and went flat as shock and pain met him straight on. Stunned, and again from some inner direction, he rolled over, came to his knees, triggered a second shot at the outlaw leader.

Through blurring vision he saw Kilrain sinking slowly, head sagged forward, arms limp. The outlaw hung motionless for a fraction of time, as the second bullet ripped into him, and then toppled stiffly.

Bobby Joe. . . . There was still Bobby Joe. . . . By the general store. . . .

The thought hammered dully in Starbuck's clouded brain. He dragged himself upright with effort. His whole right side was numb, seemed not to be a part of him. Gathering strength, he started for the street, continuing the course he had been taking when he encountered Con Kilrain.

He was going the wrong direction. . . . Bobby Joe was not that way — not toward the hotel. He was farther up — the store. . . .

Reasoning stumbled about in his flagging mind, finally registered. Reversing himself, he cut back for the rear of the sagging shack. He gained the corner, began an unsteady turn, half falling in the effort. As if from a great distance behind him, he heard the crash of a pistol. Roaring pain seared again through his body, driving him down.

He fired twice at the vague, weaving shadow he saw running toward him — Bobby Joe. He knew that it was him because of the sun shining on the silver buckle he was wearing. *My buckle!*

The dim shadow halted abruptly, staggered to one side, fell. Starbuck, at the stage where pain was so massive as to be an anesthetic, stared woodenly at the prone figure. Muttering incoherently, he dragged himself to where the outlaw lay face up, sightless eyes staring into the brassy arch of the sky. Somewhere he could hear a voice calling, crying his name. . . . Hetty's voice he thought, but he couldn't be sure.

Fumbling, working at it doggedly, he released the tongue of the buckle, freed the belt encircling Bobby Joe's waist. With great effort he pulled it clear. He looked up wearily at the blur of faces that suddenly were all around him.

"I'm taking this," he mumbled thickly. "Happens to — be — mine," and then accepted gratefully the smothering fog of blackness that welled up from nowhere to block out all pain and thought and engulf him in unconsciousness.

☆ 23 ☆

It was Simon Pierce who touched off the blaze. Standing bareheaded in the blistering Texas sun, the empty sleeve of his homespun shirt neatly folded and pinned, he dropped the burning fagot into a pile of dry twigs and stepped back.

No cheers went up from the members of the Family scattered about him in a loose half circle. All watched silently, seeing in his act the foretelling of death for a faith and belief that had seen them and their forebears through many trying days.

As the flames surged upward, ravaging the juiceless branches and leaves camouflaging the barrier that had turned aside all would-be newcomers to the valley, Starbuck glanced about. The ceremony was partly for his benefit, he realized; but also it was meant to impress the younger Hebrenites with the fact that the future for them was to be different.

Grasping the headstall of the horse beside him — a black that had once borne the weight of Con Kilrain — he steadied the nervous animal as the fire crackled fiercely. He'd turn the animal in to the first lawman he could find, buy himself another. Chances were the black had been stolen by the outlaw and Shawn had no wish to be strung up for a horsethief.

Three weeks — twenty-two days to be exact — had slipped by since the showdown in the village, time during which it had been touch and go for him while he fretted under the constant ministrations of the Hebrenite women who were determined that not only would he recover but also that he would heal unblemished from the outlaw bullets that had smashed into him.

And he had. What had been told to him concerning the medical and surgical skill of the women was true; he was as fit as the day he stumbled onto the secret valley.

But it was secret no more. He had brought change, and he was seeing the proof of it now in the leaping flames consuming the gate that had sealed off the canyon and the broad valley beyond it for so many years.

"We ain't aiming to keep folks out no more," Micah Jones said, turning to him. "We're going to welcome them, invite them to make a home here."

"Not that we're giving up the things we've been taught," Pierce, who was now the Senior Elder of the sect, added. "We figure our way's still the best — that violence is wrong and turning from it is what folks should do. We'll offer our ways to those who come. If they see fit to accept them, well and good. If not, it's their right and we'll try to understand."

"What about your young people?" Shawn asked, glancing to where Hetty stood with several others in the shade of a small cottonwood. She was smiling and talking animatedly.

"They can stay, or they can go — when they're of proper age. It's to be their choice. But with new folks moving into the valley, we don't think they'll be wanting to leave."

Shawn agreed. The cattle drivers, along with the teamsters, had returned some days back. Enroute they had encountered a wagon train headed west. A rider had been dispatched to intercept the emigrants, tell them of the valley and invite them to settle on its fertile slopes. The offer had been accepted, and now everyone anxiously awaited the train's arrival.

Starbuck looped the reins over the black's neck, toed the stirrup, and swung into the saddle. Those same teamsters had answered his question regarding Hagerman's Hash Knife Ranch and the Carazones Peaks country; of Hagerman they could tell him nothing, but the Carazones Peaks — southeast and a long hundred miles away.

Settling himself, he glanced around at the faces of his friends, smiled at Hetty who paused, touched him with a soft look, and resumed her conversing. Simon Pierce stepped up, solemnly offered his hand.

"I'm speaking for all the Family — come back. There'll always be a place here for you."

Starbuck nodded. "Just might take you up on

that someday," he replied, and again letting his gaze slip over the small crowd, he rode the black through the now open mouth of the canyon.

Someday . . . maybe . . . after he'd found Ben. It could be soon. . . . Ben just might be at Hagerman's ranch. . . .